Praise for
New York Times and USA Today Bestselling Author

Diane Capri

"Full of thrills and tension, but smart and human, too."
Lee Child, #1 New York Times Bestselling Author of Jack Reacher Thrillers

"[A] welcome surprise....[W]orks from the first page to 'The End'."
Larry King

"Swift pacing and ongoing suspense are always present...[L]ikable protagonist who uses her political connections for a good cause...Readers should eagerly anticipate the next [book]."
Top Pick, Romantic Times

"...offers tense legal drama with courtroom overtones, twisty plot, and loads of Florida atmosphere. Recommended."
Library Journal

"[A] fast-paced legal thriller...energetic prose...an appealing heroine...clever and capable supporting cast...[that will] keep readers waiting for the next [book]."
Publishers Weekly

"Expertise shines on every page."
Margaret Maron, Edgar, Anthony, Agatha and Macavity Award Winning MWA Past President

HIT THE ROAD
JACK

by DIANE CAPRI

Published by: AugustBooks
http://www.AugustBooks.com

First Print Edition
ISBN-13: 978-1-940768-08-3

Original cover design by Cory Clubb
Interior formatting by Author E.M.S.

Published in the United States of America.

Visit the author website:
http://www.DianeCapri.com

ALSO BY DIANE CAPRI

For Lee Child,
with unrelenting gratitude.

CONTENTS

Dear Friends,

It's an honor and a pleasure to write for you. Many of you found me because of my connection to my great friend, Lee Child, and the spin off books I'm writing on the hunt for Jack Reacher. This collection is for especially for you.

Like many authors working today, both Lee and I publish ebooks more frequently than "tree" books. Many readers enjoy tree books and also collect them. So when readers asked for a collection of my novellas and also asked me to publish them in print as well as electronic versions, I was thrilled to oblige.

What I've packaged for you here, never before collected together in electronic form and never before in print, are three Hunt for Jack Reacher Series novellas as well as two Hunt for Justice Series novellas. I hope you enjoy these tales as much as I enjoyed writing them for you.

If you love this collection, please leave a review at the retailer where you bought the book and anywhere else you think readers might see it. Your reviews really help other readers to decide whether or not to give my books a chance.

Now sit back in your easy chair with your favorite beverage close at hand and dive in while I get back to work on more new books especially for you, the best readers in the world. One of these days, I hope to meet you and say thank you in person. Until then—

Caffeinate and Carry On!

Best,

Diane

p.s. I hope you're on my email list, where we let you know about new books, opportunities, contests, giveaways, and, well everything first and exclusively. I certainly don't want to leave you out! (And don't worry -- I'll never, ever send you any spam. If it's email from me, you can be sure it's got something terrific to offer.) If you're not signed up and you'd like to be you can do that here: http://dianecapri.com/get-involved/get-my-newsletter/.

JACK

IN A BOX

CHAPTER ONE

FBI SPECIAL AGENT KIM Otto's slowly descending eyelids abraded like forty-grit sandpaper along her corneas and rested briefly before ascending in gouging retraction. How long had she been sitting here? The FBI headquarters building was quiet here in the basement. Activity was limited to higher floors where essential matters were handled.

"What are you missing?" she asked the empty room as if she expected the answer to be revealed, when she expected nothing of the sort. If she was going to find anything at all, she'd have found it long before now. But she couldn't give up, so she thought it through again.

She'd begun by searching for general information. Finding none, she'd narrowed her search to the fingerprints. Fingerprints never changed, never disappeared, never failed to identify. Every law enforcement officer knew a fingerprint was worth a thousand eyewitness reports and often better even than DNA.

But, like DNA, fingerprints were only useful when compared to known identities. Law enforcement files around the globe were filled with unidentified prints and DNA. The first order of business was to find proof of positive identity. She'd thought that would be easy. Wrong.

Jack Reacher must have been fingerprinted by the Army, like every other soldier. Maybe a single set of prints made all those years ago could have been misplaced in the days before computers ruled the world. Or maybe accidentally destroyed somehow.

Kim thought not.

Relevant military files were integrated with FBI and other agency files now, she knew. But Reacher's army discharge was long before 9/11. Back in those days, government agencies didn't share information in the way they did now. Some old files involving military personnel instead of criminal defendants were not searchable in the various FBI databases Kim had the necessary security clearance to examine without raising the alarms she didn't want to trigger.

Her plan was to check the military files last because they were the oldest. Her accounting background led her to prioritize the most recent information first, or first in, last out.

Reacher wasn't an army grunt who'd been drafted, served a quick term, and mustered out. He'd spent thirteen years in service to his country, including his last stint with the military police. As an MP his reference fingerprints would have been routinely used to exclude his prints from those left by witnesses and suspects at crime scenes.

Kim should have found at least a few Reacher exemplars in the FBI databases. But she hadn't.

Nor had she really expected to find anything relevant, although she hadn't abandoned all hope. But her realistic plan was only to confirm her assumption that nothing concerning Jack Reacher existed in FBI files. After that, she and Gaspar could move on to conducting additional interviews with victims, witnesses, reporting parties, and informants. Always assuming they could find any of the above.

"Coffee. You need a caffeine jolt," Kim said aloud.

She stood, eyes closed to avoid the gouging, stretched like a cat, then a downward dog, working the kinks out of her stiff muscles. She heard nothing but her own breathing. She stretched her neck and shoulders again before making her way to the elevator in search of java, nectar of the gods.

Kim pressed the elevator button and completed another round of stretches while she waited. Lights above the door flashed up and down and up and down, stopping at floors high above. The basement was low priority, below stops where others were consumed by important activity, Kim concluded. The only coffee at this hour would be inside the busiest sectors of the building, places she didn't want to be seen. Yet... She sighed, shrugged, headed for the stairs.

When she exited on the ground floor her personal cell phone vibrated. She checked the caller ID before answering.

"Good morning, Dad. You're up early."

CHAPTER TWO

FBI SPECIAL AGENT CARLOS Gaspar had planned to leave early even before the classified envelope arrived containing nothing but a copy of Major Jack (none) Reacher's formal headshot; on the back, a time and place for a meeting.

Had Reacher planned the meet? Or was it someone else who wanted Otto and Gaspar present? Either way, the big question was why?

Nothing traceable about the envelope or its contents. He chased down the delivery service but got no further data. The headshot was easily obtainable by any number of people. Hell, he'd been supplied one just like it when he initially received the Reacher file assignment.

The time and place for the meet was a bit out of the ordinary, but not alarming. The National Gallery of Art, East Building, on Pennsylvania Avenue. Ten o'clock tonight. It would be dark but not deserted. The building was one of those modern designs full of angles and shadows suitable for clandestine activities. But not a bad neighborhood, unless you hated politicians, and the entire town was infested with those.

He'd tried to call Otto, but her plane was already in the air and flying straight into an early winter storm. She hated flying under the best conditions; she'd be too wired by the storm and her errand to make any sense, even if he'd reached her. They'd talk tonight. In D.C.

Fifty minutes before he planned to depart, his bag was packed and stowed in the Crown Vic's trunk. He'd dressed in his Banana Republic suit. Gaspar popped another Tylenol, rested on the chaise lounge, and watched his youngest daughter from behind mirrored sunglasses that reflected little of Miami's winter sunlight and none of its heat.

Today was Angela's fifth birthday, meaning five giggling girls had invaded his home overnight. That was one of his wife's rules. No sleepovers until age five, then five girls for her fifth birthday, six for the next, and so on. His eldest would be thirteen in a few months; the idea raised gooseflesh along his arms and not only because thirteen teenagers in his small house would be ear splitting.

Thirteen was a dangerous age. Rebellion. Independence. Sex. He clearly recalled himself and his buddies at thirteen. The prospect of launching his firstborn daughter into that realm terrified him, but he acted as if it didn't. He shrugged. No way to stop the clock. It is what it is.

Gaspar felt his eyelids slide closed and shoved them up again. Yes, he was tired, but that was nothing new. Exhaustion had been a constant companion since his injury. He rarely slept more than an hour before throbbing pain in his right side awakened him. He'd become a quick-nap expert to capture missing sleep, but he felt his senses dulled, his reaction times slowed. The healed scrape where a bullet had seared his abdomen burned like a rash, reminding him to stay alert. He was grateful to have the fearless Otto as his partner, a solid assignment, and damn lucky to be alive to see his daughters' birthdays.

Cacophonous noise drowned such thinking. Five girls cavorting in the backyard pool, squeals, shouts, splashes. Surely decibel level ordinances in Miami's residential neighborhoods were violated. He'd tried asking them to quiet down, and they did, but joy erupted again louder than ever after maybe five subdued seconds. Was impulse control equal to age? Would the quiet seconds lengthen to six and then seven? Would it be five more years before he might enjoy ten seconds of silence at home from his youngest girl?

He'd survived many life-threatening situations, but fathering frightened him more than anything. Four daughters already and his wife pregnant with a boy. Job one was keeping his family safe.

Before his injury he never considered such things, never worried that he'd fail, never gnawed the consequences. Maria had handled the girls effortlessly and he'd swooped in to count noses and grab hugs before bedtime. Confidence had oozed from Gaspar's pores back then. Four kids hadn't seemed overwhelming. He hadn't felt boxed in so much as engulfed by creatures he loved more than anything.

Not anymore. Adding a fifth child at this point terrified him. A boy. Boys needed a solid role model, a strong father like his own had been, but Gaspar's body refused to perform as required and he could barely keep his head in the game.

How would Maria manage the girls and a new baby while he worked the Reacher file, traveled all over the country, only coming home for brief stints, not knowing how long this assignment would go on, worried that the work would end too soon?

He shrugged again without realizing he'd moved this time. It was what it was.

As Otto said, only one choice. He'd do what he had to do.

Men work. Husbands work. Fathers work.

He had to work.

They needed the money.

Twenty years to go. Simple as that.

But he'd bought a big life insurance policy. Just in case.

CHAPTER THREE

FBI SPECIAL AGENT KIM Otto had made a quick dash to
Wisconsin over the weekend because Grandma Louisa Otto
was dying. Not shocking, given her age. Modern medicine
had pulled her through heart arrhythmias, osteoporosis,
micro-strokes, and cancer, twice. This time she'd had another
heart attack.

Kim doubted Grandma Louisa would actually die. Ever.
Pure German stubbornness had kept her alive more than 102
years. Kim figured she had inherited the stubborn gene from
Louisa.

But if death was to happen, Kim didn't want to be there to
see it. She was not comforted by bodies in coffins or funerals or
memorial services and avoided them whenever possible.
Closure? Humbug.

"God knows how much longer she'll last, Kim," her
father said, probably noticing Kim's lack of enthusiasm for
the trip.

"Is mom going?" Kim asked. Her stomach was already
churning at no prospect of playing referee between Grandma

Louisa and Sen Li. Kim reached into her pocket for an antacid and slipped it under her tongue.

"We've been there all week. We'll return Monday," Dad replied, subdued. "Just go to Frankenmuth, honey. Say goodbye while you still can. You'll be glad you did."

In what universe?

Still, her father rarely asked her for anything. Sen Li had drilled into her children from infancy—when there's only one choice, it's the right choice.

So she went.

Just in case.

Kim had flown out early, before she could chicken out. Adding two plane flights to her life was never her first choice, but too often it was her only option.

Miraculously, the plane didn't crash and she made it to Madison in one piece. Frankenmuth Otto Regional Hospital was a twenty-mile cab ride from the airport. She'd booked a two o'clock flight back to D.C. God willing, she'd arrive at Reagan National by five-thirty. Plenty of time to take care of the things she needed to do before she met Gaspar Sunday. Get in, get out. That was her plan.

This could work, she thought, right up until the cab dropped her at the hospital's front entrance, when her internal response became, again, *In what universe?*

Nothing ever worked according to plan where her family was concerned. Dad had said he and his five siblings were posting a constant bedside vigil for Grandma Louisa, who had been a widow for decades. Kim shouldn't have been surprised to see the line of Ottos, all blonde and oversized, that snaked down the block from the hospital's entrance.

Mid-November was bleakly cold in Frankenmuth,

Wisconsin. Men, women, and kids alike wore jeans, boots, and sweatshirts under coats, hats, and gloves. Practical, comfortable clothes. The kind Kim favored when she wasn't dressed for work. After all, she was German and oversized herself on the inside.

Only Kim's father had strayed from the family farm in Wisconsin, and he had traveled to neighboring Michigan at figurative gunpoint because his parents had refused to welcome his pregnant Vietnamese wife.

These Ottos served their community as farmers, shopkeepers, teachers, nurses, military, and a few, like Kim, were cops of one kind or another. Otto cousins lined up today because they worked during the week and Sunday was reserved for church.

Kim paid the cab driver and nodded to her cousins as she walked back to take her place at the end of the line. Shivering began immediately. Her suit was too thin a barrier for the Wisconsin wind. She turned up the jacket collar, stuffed her hands into the pockets, and shifted her weight from one foot to the other, attempting to gin up some body heat. The strategy didn't work well. Soon, the snowy concrete had transferred its glacial cold upward through the soles of her shoes.

Eventually, Kim reached the interior waiting room that had been overtaken by the Otto clan. She was in no hurry to approach Louisa's sickbed. She left the line and stood in a corner near the heat vent.

She absorbed the warmth through her pores while the noxious citrus-scented air purifier attacked her sinuses, causing a sharp pain between her eyebrows at the bridge of her slender nose.

She was too cold to make conversation, but no one spoke

much at all, and certainly not to her. Which was just fine. She felt as much an overwhelmed fish out of water as she always had among her fair-haired, blue-eyed, giant-sized cousins. None of the right-sized Ottos were older than eight and their conversational abilities would probably be all about age-appropriate video games anyway. The Ottos rarely spoke to her under normal circumstances; no reason to change things now. Kim shrugged.

As a child she'd wondered what it would feel like to be welcomed into this big, warm family. A long time ago, she'd realized she would never know that feeling. Every family needed its flock of black sheep. She was a Michigan Otto, born on the wrong side of the blanket as far as the Wisconsin Ottos were concerned. Period. End of story. She shrugged again. It was what it was.

A low murmur from the group interrupted Kim's thoughts and drew her glance toward the doorway. Attired in a full dress blue Class A Army uniform complete with ribbons, hat in hand, another Otto had entered the waiting area. Only one Otto was currently serving in the Army at that level, and only one Otto would compel the immediate respect that settled palpably over the room.

Kim had seen him maybe three times in her life before today and never in uniform, but she recognized Captain Lothar Otto instantly.

Literally the fair-haired boy of the moment, he sported the unmistakable Otto family countenance, complete with caterpillar eyebrows and what Kim's father called a high, intelligent forehead, also known as a rapidly receding hairline. He'd grown up in Frankenmuth like all the normal Ottos, attended West Point, and then served the Army and fought in its wars. She'd heard he'd been wounded two years ago, but he looked fit enough today.

Ottos were not a demonstrative bunch by nature and Kim observed Lothar make the obligatory rounds seeming no more comfortable than she would have been. Men shook his hand or saluted respectfully; women nodded and smiled or saluted; children kept their distance and saluted.

Lothar's identification was positively confirmed when he passed close enough for Kim to read his nametag, but he merely nodded toward her without stopping or noticing whether she nodded in reply. She didn't mind; she was no better at small talk than the rest of her family. She did not salute.

When Kim had absorbed enough real warmth to feel her toes again, she became aware of the lateness of the hour. She needed to do what she'd come for and get back to Madison for her flight back to DC.

Yet the neverending line of Ottos continued unabated toward Grandma Louisa's room. When she could stall no longer, Kim joined the cousin trail, feeling as if the guillotine waited at the end of the line. The piercing pain between her eyes made the prospect of losing her head almost welcome.

Kim shuffled along with the line advancing at warp speed of two feet a minute, closing the distance in an orderly fashion as each cousin slipped into the sick room alone and stayed precisely sixty seconds before emerging without flowing tears or evidence of sobbing via fists-full of damp, crumpled tissues. Lack of hysteria salved Kim's anxiety; the inexorable forward movement did not.

Grandma Louisa had never inspired open affection from anyone and Kim wondered how she coped when her stoic progeny remained composed. Did Grandma think no one cared?

Or was she, herself uncaring? This mystery had plagued Kim most of her life. Was it she who felt nothing for Grandma first? Or, as a small child, had she absorbed the message that Grandma Louisa felt nothing for her and defended against apathy thereafter?

Kim sighed and raised her hand to knead tension from the back of her neck. Again, she was glad Sen Li was absent. Mom would have created a spectacle of some kind about the Otto family's cold nature, the way she always did, and Kim had no desire to cope with such scenes on top of everything else. At the moment, Kim couldn't recall the precise nature of their last battle. None of it mattered any more. The old lady was on her way out. Whatever the source of their problems, now was the time to set them aside and move on.

Hushed words hummed quietly among the cousins at volumes too low to comprehend, Kim realized. She was sure the conversations were about crops and kids and church and plans for Thanksgiving. Nothing she would feel comfortable discussing with these near strangers, even if they tried to include her, which they did not. Not that it mattered. She'd be gone soon, and so would Grandma Louisa.

Too quickly, the Otto in front of her entered Grandma's room. The door closed quietly behind him. Kim was next and she had no idea what she'd say. She had not seen Grandma Louisa for ten years and the last time they'd met ended badly, as had most of their encounters. Grandma Louisa could not forgive Sen Li for taking Albert away from the family. That grudge engulfed Albert's daughters because they resembled their mother. Kim had accepted years ago that she would never be tall and blonde and German on the outside; it wasn't enough for Grandma Louisa that Kim was as fierce as any Otto on the inside.

Swiftly, the door opened, the cousin came out, looked Kim in the eye and said, "You're up. Good luck."

Kim considered whether it was too late to run, but she stood as tall as a four-foot-eleven-and-a-half-inch, ninety-nine pound Asian-American woman could stand, squared her shoulders and marched past the threshold, checking for a quick escape route, but finding none. Someone pushed the door and it sucked solidly shut behind her.

Grandma Louisa's bed filled most of the room. An oxygen cannula rested in her nose but otherwise she'd changed not one iota since the last time Kim had seen her. She wore a pink brocade bed jacket, her gray hair was teased and lacquered as usual, and her hands were folded on her lap, the better to display her rings and manicured nails. She wore pearl and sapphire earrings and a double strand of pearls around her sizeable neck. Mauve lipstick emphasized her still-full lips. Blush rosied her cheeks. Stylish eyeglasses rested on her nose visually enlarging her blue eyes to bowl size.

Louisa Otto, matriarch of the Frankenmuth Ottos, held court as she always had, as if she were not just the head of one sizeable but important farming community, but Empress Augusta herself.

Whoever had closed the door gave Kim a little shove in the small of her back, prodding her closer to the bed.

"Kimmy," Louisa said, a moment before she reached out with a strong claw, restraining Kim by engulfing her hand inside a big fist, holding tight. Rough callouses on Louisa's palm scraped Kim's skin.

Perhaps Grandma Louisa was near death, but she seemed a lot more alive than Kim had been led to believe.

"You look great," Kim said, clearing her throat and covering surprise as she leaned over to kiss a papery cheek dotted with lipstick from previous kissers.

Grandma Louisa replied, "I really do, don't I?"

Kim had to laugh. What could she possibly say in reply?

Not that Grandma Louisa gave her a chance. Maybe Kim's mind had misplaced the facts of their last argument, but Louisa's had not. She launched again as if the dispute had concluded ten minutes ago, not ten years ago. "Kimmy, I want to see you married to a good German Lutheran before I die. A baby on the way. Maybe two."

"You'll need to live a good long while then, Grandma," Kim said, struggling to eliminate annoyance from her tone as the old feelings flooded back. They'd fought bitterly ten years ago because Grandma had arranged such a union for Kim and Kim had secretly married already, not to a German Lutheran but to a Vietnamese immigrant. Kim was divorced now, but she simply refused to have any part of the old tyrant's nosey meddling.

"I will if you will," Grandma Louisa said flatly, steely-eyed and uncompromising. She squeezed Kim's hand tighter before releasing her completely. "Now would be a good time to find good husband material before you leave Wisconsin. I've lined up a few prospects for you to see this afternoon back at my house."

Kim felt anger bubbling up from her now toasty feet, rising to levels that would have the family comparing her to Sen Li, and not favorably. Kim clamped her jaws closed and replied, "Thanks. I'm on my way."

She didn't say on her way where.

Grandma Louisa beamed as if she'd settled the fortunes of the crown princess. "You'll be glad when you're settled, Kimmy. Like your cousins."

Damn that woman!

Kim said nothing. She glanced at the uncles standing on either side of their mother, but neither could muster the guts to meet her gaze. She nodded, pulled her hand away, turned and left the room, saving thirty seconds for the next cousin in line, who was also single and probably wouldn't thank her for the extra time.

No one seemed to notice when Kim continued walking, out of the waiting room, down the hallway, and left the hospital through the front exit where Otto cousins continued to throng the entrance.

She stood at the cabstand and fumed, muttering suitable rejoinders to the old bat under her breath and louder epithets in her head. She barely noticed the frigid outside air for the first five minutes while the heat of her rage kept adrenaline pumping.

Where are the damned taxis?

Too quickly, the cold bulldozed into her bones. She hunched inside her suit jacket, stomped her feet to knock the snow away from her soles and keep her circulation going. It was freezing out here. Even colder than Grandma Louisa, if that was possible.

Why in the name of God didn't you bring a coat and boots? Better yet, why didn't you just say no, Dad, I'm not going. Not now. Not ever. Forget it.

Ranting didn't heat the atmosphere even one degree.

Global warming, my ass.

Kim felt her corneas might frost. She squeezed her eyes shut and shivered a bit more attempting to raise her body temperature. She wasn't going back inside to wait, even if her feet froze to the sidewalk and her eyelids ice-glued themselves together.

She heard the growl of an engine and opened her eyes expecting to see a yellow cab. Instead, a black SUV had pulled up alongside, Captain Lothar Otto at the wheel. He lowered the passenger window and said, "I'm headed toward the airport. Can I drop you somewhere?"

Kim wasted no body heat demurring. She hopped up into the passenger seat and immediately put her frozen fingers near the blasting heat vent.

"Frontier?" she said.

"Nonstop, huh? You can't be afraid of flying." When she failed to reply, he said, "Jumping out of moving planes, now that's a lot harder." Still no response. He took a deep breath. "Okay then. Dane County, Frontier Airlines it is." Lothar attended to driving the heavy vehicle expertly down snow-covered streets through towns unprepared for the early winter storm.

After she'd warmed up enough to sit a normal distance from the fan's blasting heat, Lothar glanced toward her and asked, "Did she give you the business about getting married and having babies before she dies?"

Kim nodded. She didn't know this man. She had no intention of discussing her personal life with him, no matter how angry she was.

He grinned. "She does that to me every time I see her."

"Really? I thought it was only me she subjected to never-ending ridicule."

Lothar laughed, the kind of deep belly laugh that only emerged from genuine mirth, the contagious kind. "When did you get so special?"

Kim smiled, felt better, almost as if she'd found an Otto family ally for the first time in her life, knowing the feeling was supremely foolish. Relief lasted about twenty seconds before the SUV swerved on a black ice patch and she grabbed the armrest to avoid being slung across the seat. She snugged up her seatbelt several notches.

Traffic slogged along, slowing their progress. Several vehicles less suited to the conditions slipped on patches of invisible black ice. They'd dodged two fender-benders already. Snow plows and salt trucks clogged the roadway, but drivers willingly waited as they passed.

Lothar concentrated intently on driving, but he must have sensed her anxiety because he said, "Planes take off in these conditions all the time around here. They'll de-ice. Two or three times if they need to. You'll be fine."

Kim's stomach started doing backflips and the two antacids she held on her tongue weren't helping in the least. De-icing two or three times? Seriously? Didn't these people know how dangerous ice on airplanes was? Didn't they understand that de-icing two or three times made crashing more likely, not less? Was she completely surrounded by hostiles here?

When they reached the curbside drop off for Frontier Airlines, Lothar turned toward her and placed a hand on her arm. "Hang on a minute. I have something for you."

Kim knew she looked puzzled because that was how she felt. Lothar reached inside his jacket and pulled a photograph from his breast pocket. He handed it to her.

She bit her lip to suppress a gasp. Major Jack Reacher's official Army headshot. She flipped the photo over and on the back was a sticker sporting typewritten information: Tonight. 10:00 p.m. National Gallery of Art, East Building, front entrance.

"What is this?"

"Following orders."

"What do you mean?"

"I was ordered to deliver that to you."

"By whom?"

"The point is someone wants to see you. They knew I could deliver the message. You understand?"

"Spell it out for me," she said, but she knew. She wanted him to voice her concern aloud so she would know she wasn't crazy. Because it was crazy to think that someone would manipulate her father to manipulate her to come to Wisconsin to meet a reliable cousin to give her a meeting back in Washington D.C. which is where she started from this morning and where she was returning in thirty-three minutes if she survived her flight.

Lothar asked a question instead. "You recognized the photo, didn't you? How are you involved with that guy? Is he the reason you were so incensed at Grandma Louisa's meddling in your personal life? You're not dating that guy?"

He seemed genuinely concerned about her, which worried her more than the message. No one in the extended Otto family had shown her the least bit of concern her entire life. Why start now?

She said, "Do *you* know him?"

"By reputation. Otherwise, before my time. Reacher was discharged in 1997. Something hinky about it, though. His situation was definitely not normal, Kim. Wherever that guy went, bodies piled up. And I'm not talking about normal battlefield casualties. Nobody is that unlucky."

"What do you mean?"

"I'm a Captain in the U.S. Army. Like you, Agent Otto, I follow orders and don't ask questions, or I pay the consequences. Before today, I never had a problem with that because the Army never ordered me to do anything this odd; something not right is going on here."

No shit, she thought. "Like what?"

He shrugged, giving up. "Friends come and go in life, but enemies pile up. Reacher made a lot of enemies. You be careful, little cuz, or you'll never reach Grandma Louisa's age with or without those Vietnamese longevity genes."

A vehicle behind the SUV laid on the horn, letting Lothar know it was long past time to move.

Kim slipped Reacher's photo into her jacket pocket, popped open the door, and slid out to the ground.

Before she closed herself outside in the cold, Lothar said, "You need anything, here's my card. I feel responsible for you now. Don't let them be calling me to your funeral."

CHAPTER FOUR

WASHINGTON, D.C. WAS FULL of shadowy men these days. Some were harmless. Some were crazy. Sometimes it was impossible to tell the difference. Always safer to avoid confrontation, just in case.

He stood motionless in a shadowed doorway, an intimidating giant, waiting. He carried his broad frame tall and straight. He wore indigo jeans and brown work boots on his feet. Both hands were stuffed into leather jacket pockets for warmth. Fair hair fell shaggy around his ears and collar, his only cap against winter's cold. Sunglasses covered his eyes and reflected the weak sunset like cat pupils. Without visible effort, he seemed infinitely patient, self-possessed, self-confident, alert and relaxed, harmless and dangerous.

Few pedestrians raised their heads from the biting November wind enough to notice him; those who did veered wide, walked along the curb, as far away as possible from the boxy doorway. Just in case.

When the burner cell phone vibrated he pulled it out of his pocket and held the speaker to his ear. The woman's voice reported just the facts, "Messages delivered; on their way."

He said nothing.

He dropped the phone to the concrete, smashed it casually with the heel of his heavy boot, picked up the largest pieces, scattered the smallest, and walked unhurried toward Pennsylvania Avenue, dropping the rest into random trash bins along his route.

CHAPTER FIVE

AGENT CARLOS GASPAR FLASHED his badge at the entrance to the Pentagon, provided appropriate identification and after his approved visitor status was confirmed, he was flagged through.

As he expected, the building was busy even though it was five o'clock on a Saturday afternoon. Gaspar had slept an hour on the plane; Tylenol, the strongest painkiller he allowed himself, never lasted longer. He'd stopped for coffee after he passed security.

No one knew him here, but both civilians and military personnel were busy with more pressing matters. He'd passed security so they ignored him, likely accepting that his clearance was high enough. Which it was.

He glanced at the digital clock on the wall. Two hours before he'd meet Otto in the coffee shop. Plenty of time.

The first step in any follow-up investigation was to review and analyze all the previous reports. Because Otto and Gaspar were tasked by one of the FBI's most powerful leaders and assigned a rush under-the-radar project, this step hadn't been completed.

He knew where he was going, what to look for, and what he should find there.

He also knew he wouldn't find it. The absence of what should be present would speak volumes.

Archived service records, defined as records for veterans sixty-two years or more post-separation, were stored and open to the public at the new National Personnel Records Center in St. Louis, Missouri. Nothing pertaining to Reacher would be archived there because he'd been discharged in March 1997.

All inactive personnel records for veterans with a discharge date less than sixty-two years ago remained the property of the Department of Defense and its individual branches. In Reacher's case, that meant the Army.

Gaspar was an active, practicing Catholic. He believed in divine providence. At first, it felt like he was on the right investigative path and he might find what he sought, even without an official archive. A fire had destroyed service records at the prior St. Louis center in 1973, but Reacher was only thirteen then.

But then Gaspar ran into several official gaps that concealed Reacher's history more effectively than youth or fire.

The Army didn't begin retaining records electronically until 2002, five years after Reacher's separation. This meant his files weren't retained in electronic format by the Army or electronically shared with the NPRC.

Worse, the Army's policies on maintaining and releasing service records were changed in April, 1997 and several times thereafter. The rules filled more than fifty-five pages, regularly revised, of course.

All of which meant that Reacher's records were once and should remain hard copies, resting in files owned by the Army that could be and probably were buried so deep in bullshit that no one would ever find them.

Unless.

Unless Reacher did something to get himself inscribed by bits and bytes into the electronic records after he left the army.

Which, Gaspar was betting, Reacher had done. Probably many times. For sure, at least once barely six months after the army let him go. If Gaspar could find that record, he'd have verified hard proof and Reacher's trail might begin to unravel.

Gaspar knew Reacher had been arrested in Margrave, Georgia, and his fingerprints were taken and sent to FBI headquarters. A report was returned to the Margrave Police Department. Margrave PD records were also destroyed in a fire, which Gaspar was as sure as he could possibly be was no coincidence.

Even so, the initial fingerprint request should exist in FBI files. Gaspar had checked. The request did not exist in FBI files. Which Gaspar was sure, but could not prove, was no coincidence, either.

This was where the government's redundancy and repetitive nature might be harnessed, Gaspar hoped. The Margrave PD request and FBI reply should also have been noted in Reacher's military file, as should any request and reply about Reacher at any time from the date of his discharge until this very moment and into the future. Anything after 2002 should be electronically recorded for sure. And anything before 1997 might also have been updated because of the later electronic entries.

It was this army record Gaspar sought now. Positive paper trail proof of the legally admissible kind that Jack Reacher had been present in Margrave in September 1997, six months after his Army discharge, that Reacher was *there.* Not a shadow. Not a ghost. Not a rumor. But a real person.

Tangible proof of Reacher's Margrave presence was important because it provided the immovable, rock hard foundation Gaspar needed to nail down. His training said it was required and his gut said it mattered and that was enough for him. He and Otto were assigned to build the Reacher file and by God, he'd do it right, and he wouldn't make his wife a widow or his five children orphans in the process if he could possibly help it.

First things first. The Margrave PD print request and the Army's reply.

Then they would take the next steps.

Whatever those steps were.

And if the print request and reply documents were missing from the army files?

Starting here and now, he would confirm one way or the other.

Gaspar was a practicing Catholic. He believed in divine intervention. But he was an FBI Special Agent who also believed in hard proof and his gut. So he knew. He knew before he opened the box marked Jack (none) Reacher and sifted through the paperwork.

Relevant records ended when Reacher separated from the army in March 1997.

After Gaspar confirmed it, he and Otto could move forward. But to where?

CHAPTER SIX

AN HOUR BEFORE THE scheduled meeting, Otto and Gaspar stepped out of the coffee shop located across the street from the J. Edgar Hoover building into the mild autumn weather. Full dark had fallen awhile back, but streetlights and headlights and floodlights eliminated all blackness. The trees were partially clothed in fall finery; grass remained green and a few flowers still bloomed. No breeze ruffled to cool the temperature.

After Wisconsin, Kim found the evening weather pleasantly warm. After Miami, Gaspar might have been a bit chilled. Both were energized by the anticipated confrontation. Maybe they were finally going to catch a break.

Saturday night on Pennsylvania Avenue NW was subdued. Traffic moved at posted speeds or less. Couples and small groups populated the sidewalks, strolling with discrete distances between them. Nothing out of the ordinary to notice.

Gaspar stretched like a cat, asked, "Shall we walk?" and set off eastbound before she had a chance to respond.

Kim ran through the options. The Metro Stop at 7th Street was off the path, a cab wasn't worth the wait, she absolutely wasn't taking the bus, Gaspar wasn't limping, and walking always helped to organize her thoughts before a mission.

"Probably easiest, if you're up for it," Kim said, quickening her pace to reach him and keep up with his longer stride.

So they approached the National Gallery of Art's East Building the first time as any tourist might travel from FBI headquarters, hoofing less than a mile along Pennsylvania Avenue, turning right at 4th Street NW, and walking along the sidewalk opposite the East Building.

Kim had studied the building through quick online research during her return flight from Madison. Opened in 1978, it was designed by I.M. Pei, which no doubt accounted for its irregular shape and probably explained the National Honor Award from the American Institute of Architects in 1981.

Inside, the building housed modern art, research centers, and offices. Outside, it was nestled among the trees, surrounded by a six-acre contemporary sculpture garden and green space on three sides.

Although it was connected underground to the more traditional West Building where the main Gallery entrance was located, the East Building also admitted the public through a massive glass-walled entrance facing 4th Street.

Before they turned onto 4th Street, they'd seen a line of cabs and limousines at the East Building's front entrance. Kim looked inside the East Building lobby as they walked past. The room seemed stuffed to capacity. Men in tuxedoes; women in long gowns and short skirts; waiters passing trays of canapés and bubbly; a string quartet playing in the front corner. None of the noise from the party seeped out to Kim's ears.

"Some sort of charity gala?" she asked, noticing the flags on a few of the limos. "Diplomats, maybe?"

At the 4th Street and Madison Drive corner, they crossed 4th Street, turned and returned along the sidewalk closest to the East Building this time. The green space was lighted, but too dark to traverse without dogs and Tasers. They stayed on the sidewalk until they reached the opposite corner, which was technically 4th Street and Constitution.

Gaspar's gaze scanned everywhere. He said, "Three dark hoodies at three o'clock, south side, between the glass pyramids. Check it out next pass."

"Reacher?"

He wagged his head. "Too small."

"You saw the sculptures and all those narrow, open areas around the building?" she asked. What worried her were the number of deeply shadowed areas suitable for clandestine attacks. Quick death was easy to imagine and bodies could lie in those shadows for a good long time before anyone noticed.

Gaspar seemed to hear her concern. "Even if he planned this—"

"You think he didn't?"

He wagged his head. "Not Reacher's style, is it? Based on what we know? He'd come right at us if he wanted to take us out."

Kim's breath sucked in and stayed there a beat. "Why don't I find that reassuring?" she said lightly when she could speak again.

Gaspar laughed. "If he planned everything. Big if. But if he did, this is a test."

"Test of what?"

Gaspar shrugged. "Dunno. He wants to see what we'll do. Whether we'll come alone or bring an army. How long we'll wait. What we'll say. My kids call it a psych-out."

Kim said nothing, but she agreed, partly. If she'd expected to find Reacher here tonight in the shadows, she would have brought more firepower. But she thought Reacher had planned this encounter. What exactly was he up to?

CHAPTER SEVEN

ON THEIR SECOND PASS in front of the building, the limos had begun to collect their diplomats and depart. They'd pulled up in front, one at a time, orderly, their drivers knowing the drill. The glass doors opened, spilling music and party chatter into the quiet.

Kim saw the three hooded people Gaspar had spied, standing between two of the glass pyramids. They wore dark jeans, dark athletic shoes, stood with their hands in their pockets, fidgeting, but otherwise seemed to lack menace. Impossible to discern whether they were men or women. Aside from the weather being too warm for hoodies, Kim saw nothing alarming about them. Yet.

By the third pass most of the guests and all of the limos had departed. The string quartet was breaking down their equipment inside. Cabs pulled up one at a time waiting for fares. The noise level had diminished.

Kim checked her Seiko. It was ten minutes past their scheduled meet. What were they looking for? Waiting for? She had no clue, and on this point she judged Gaspar clueless as well.

Was Reacher here? Watching? Kim had looked for him but had seen nothing resembling a giant paying attention to her.

On the fourth pass, Kim noticed a woman standing apart from the building in the shadow of the largest pyramid, facing the line of cabs at the front entrance, facing her and Gaspar, facing the three hoodies, although they were blocked from her view by the large glass pyramid that separated them.

CHAPTER EIGHT

THE WOMAN WORE AN ankle-length black cape and silver party shoes with a three-inch spike heel poked below the hemline. The cape's full hood covered her head and obscured her face. She was slightly built, medium height. Kim could discern nothing else about the woman's shape concealed by her cape.

Kim felt her gun resting securely within easy reach before she touched Gaspar's arm. He nodded. They moved together into the shadows toward the woman. Despite the hour's walking, his limp remained under control.

The woman said, "No closer. I can hear you from there."

They stopped. Kim calculated how quickly she could close the distance. Slightly faster than their adversary, since she was encumbered by those spike heels.

"What do you want?" the woman asked.

"You know that already," Kim answered and then asked her own question. "Who are you?"

The woman smiled briefly, as if the response was expected according to some tit-for-tat plan. "Susan Duffy, DEA, Houston office. Why are you hunting Reacher?"

"We want information about him." Kim hesitated a couple of beats to see if the woman would fill the silence. She didn't.

"Why do you care?"

Susan Duffy broke the rules; she didn't answer the question.

"What kind of information?"

"Everything, including his underwear size and what kind of condoms he uses. Whatever we need to get him in the box," Gaspar said.

Susan Duffy, if that's who she was, laughed.

Kim was vaguely aware that the departing gala guests had diminished from a few hundred to a few dozen to a few couples, making the trek from the entrance to the waiting cabs only a pair at a time.

Gaspar asked, "What do you know about Reacher?"

Duffy had tired of the game, perhaps. She simply stated the message she'd come to deliver. "You're wasting your time looking in official files. You'll find plenty before March 1997, but it's all bullshit Reacher prepared himself. You won't find anything involving Reacher after that."

"Why not?"

Duffy's expression was unreadable. "Reacher has friends in high and low places."

"Friends who made his crimes disappear, you mean?"

Duffy's tone hardened. "Friends like me. Friends who notice you making pests of yourselves in our files and repeatedly finding nothing. You don't want that to happen again. Not everyone is as understanding as I am."

Gaspar asked, "How do you know every file has been scrubbed clean of every Jack Reacher reference?"

Duffy slid the big hood back revealing short blonde hair, small ears close to her head, and huge emerald earrings. She put

a bit of friendly into her voice. "Keep looking if you have
nothing better to do. Your file on Jack Reacher will remain thin.
Your mission will fail. You'll never put Reacher in any kind of
box. And you'll piss people off. But hey, if you want to throw
your careers in the toilet, you'll get no problem from me."

Kim watched one of the last pair of partiers walking toward
the curb while she allowed this information to soak in. Both the
man and the woman were older, a bit unsteady on their feet.
Tipsy maybe.

She didn't know how she felt about Duffy's attitude.
Challenged? Should she try to prove Duffy wrong? Or relieved?
Because she could now focus elsewhere?

She asked, "Do you know where Reacher is?"

After a moment, Duffy shook her head, "You won't find him
if he doesn't want to be found."

Gaspar's impatience flared. "We'll find him. We found
Osama Bin Laden and he was a hell of a lot more powerful than
Jack Reacher."

Duffy smiled again, "Yeah, we found Bin Laden. After
ten years of looking. Yeah, we got him. After SEAL Team
Six made it happen." She paused for the briefest of moments.
"But we didn't take him alive. If you've got ten years and a
SEAL team, maybe you can manage to kill Reacher, but you
won't take him alive unless he wants you to." She shrugged.
"Sure. Why not?"

Kim took a deep breath. "So what do you suggest?"

"You could give up."

Gaspar chuckled. "You don't know Otto."

The energy in the air seemed to shift, as if Duffy had done
what she'd come to do. She nodded slightly before lifting the
hood to cover her shimmering blonde hair and returning her

hands to her pockets. Her slight form almost merged with the darkness and became a single shadow.

"Suit yourself," her disembodied voice seemed to echo too loudly. She softened her tone. "But know this: you risk everything if you keep looking. *Everything.* And Reacher risks nothing while he waits. That doesn't sound like a winning equation to me. Does it to you?"

CHAPTER NINE

BEFORE KIM COULD ANSWER she heard a loud thump behind her. She turned to see the three hoodies emerge from the pyramids moving swiftly. They approached the older couple leaving the gala.

The hoodies' moves seemed choreographed, as if they'd practiced or maybe done this many times before. One shoved into the distinguished tuxedoed man knocking him off balance; he shouted "Hey!" before he regained his unsteady footing.

At the same time, the second hoodie stopped, raised his arm, and pointed a Glock squarely at the older woman's chest. The woman looked green, as if she might vomit, and began to shake.

The third hoodie shoved the tuxedoed man backward and shouted, "You got something to say?"

The man tripped and fell on his left side. A loud crack followed by the man's animal-like screaming confirmed broken bones, at least.

Otto pulled her weapon and aimed it at the first hoodie's center mass, and shouted, "FBI!"

Simultaneously, Gaspar pivoted on his good left leg, rushed

the gunman, and knocked him to the ground, sending his Glock skimming the sidewalk into the shadows toward Duffy. The gunman's temple slammed onto the concrete and bounced twice, leaving him splayed and motionless, his neck bent at an unnatural angle.

The older woman's horrified face lasted three seconds before she staggered, fainted, and fell face down onto the sidewalk, breaking her nose. Blood pooled and seeped into view from the center of her face.

The second hoodie froze in place, arms up, hands palm out in recognizable surrender. Security reinforcements approached running, guns drawn.

For the next moments, Otto held the two muggers at gunpoint while Gaspar attended to the woman.

Kim glanced briefly toward Duffy. For the first time, she saw a man standing alone in the sculpture's shadow. He looked familiar, but it was too dark to be sure. He was dressed in jeans and a leather jacket and work boots. Both hands were stuffed into the pockets of his jacket. He wore no hat. Duffy, completely engulfed in the long, black cape, passed close to him. He dipped his head to catch words that Kim was too far away to hear, or to be heard if she'd shouted to them.

Duffy never stopped walking. She disappeared into the darkness of the sculpture garden. The big man looked straight toward Kim long enough to cause a frisson of recognition to run up her spine before he, too, disappeared.

CHAPTER TEN

SECURITY GUARDS ARRIVED ON the scene, called for backup, secured all three hoodies, and assumed control. Minutes later, flashing lights from first responder vehicles lined up along 4th Street like a holiday parade.

Once the muggers were in custody, the tuxedoed man and older woman placed in an ambulance bound for the nearest hospital, Gaspar slipped into the shadows searching for Susan Duffy. But he found only damp November air, as Kim had known he would.

Gaspar returned, dipped his head to ask quietly, making the effort to return them to normalcy. "Now what, Boss Dragon Lady?"

"Like Duffy suggested, Zorro, we'll start where Reacher left off."

Still staring at the empty space where Duffy had been, Gaspar asked, "Which would be where, Susie Wong?"

Agent Otto turned toward Pennsylvania Avenue, smiled and replied, "We're building a file, Chico, not reading one. Think about it. Only one choice. U.S. Army buddies before March 1997."

THE END

JACK

AND KILL

For Lee Child,
with unrelenting gratitude

CHAPTER ONE

OTTO'S MOOD MATCHED THE bleak November landscape.
They'd traveled the county road for eighteen miles under
smothering gray skies, which allowed plenty of time for
brooding. Thin snow covered the empty fields like a dirty
blanket. Perhaps a riot of color had dressed the hardwoods
before Halloween, but now only a few dead leaves dangled from
dried stems beneath spindly branches. Even the vehicle in which
they traveled was dull inside and out.

She felt captured in a monochrome movie. Yet, she
welcomed the dreary weather because while the low, dense cloud
ceiling interfered with the Unmanned Aerial Vehicle
surveillance drones, she enjoyed a thin slice of breathing room.

Not the atmospheric gloom, then, but her quarry was
responsible for her personal brain cloud. He was toying with her,
which was okay. But he was winning the game, which wasn't.

"Tell me again why you think we'll find Reacher in New
Hope," she said.

FBI Special Agent Kim Louisa Otto didn't mind matching
wits with Jack (none) Reacher at the right time and place.

Actually, she hoped this assignment grew in that direction.

Meanwhile, a better profile of Reacher slowly developed in her mind the way an old-fashioned photographic image revealed itself when blank paper was submerged in the proper fluids. She was better at strategic games than he was; Reacher's military file confirmed. But preparation was key. She needed to gather sufficient data to devise and implement a decent strategic plan before their joust. In short, she needed more time.

Meaning today was most definitely not the right day. Nor was New Hope, Virginia, the right place. Which was why, despite the perfect weather for a confrontation that might escape sophisticated surveillance, she wasn't all that happy right at the moment. She didn't expect to get any happier as the day wore on, either. She expected the opposite.

Behind the wheel of the full-sized sedan he'd selected at the rental counter in DC, Gaspar sprawled deliberately. His right leg was fully extended to reduce the pain that often hobbled him. Otto had stopped counting how many Tylenols he'd swallowed already, although she worried about his liver. One of many tacit agreements they'd fallen into during their brief but intense partnership. As if not asking meant not knowing, and not knowing meant not happening.

He glanced toward her and frowned, but his tone was quiet, perhaps annoyed. "I didn't say we'd *find* him, Sunshine. We're building a file, not conducting a manhunt. I said he was *there yesterday*. Big difference."

She could tell Gaspar wanted to find Reacher today, though. "Do I want to know how you acquired that intel?"

In response, he flashed a quick stare before returning his attention to driving. Which probably meant he'd ignored their operating protocols. Again. Working a different case with different rules, he might have offered more or she might have asked. As it was, they'd agreed plausible deniability might save them if either was eventually forced to testify. Which they'd also agreed was more than likely where the whole Reacher mess was headed.

"How much farther?" she asked instead.

He glanced at the odometer. "Maybe fifteen more miles. Give or take."

The rental was equipped with GPS and they had their own equipment, too. She could find the precise distance easily enough. But GPS acted like a tracking beacon for UAVs that crosshatched the country and she'd had enough of being watched. Instead, they did most things the old-fashioned way, making every effort to remain skinny straws in the very large haystack of surveillance data. The boss and too many others had unlimited access to their movements.

Maybe Reacher did everything the old-fashioned way, too. Maybe that was how he stayed far off the grid. It seemed if anyone saw Reacher it was not because they found him but because Reacher found them. Otto had begun to envy Reacher's expertise in privacy protection. He was exceedingly adept at secrets, too. Otto's experience said a guy that good at secrets had way too much to hide.

This county road would take them directly into town and no amount of reviewing their route would make the drive less desolate.

Kim murmured her thoughts aloud. "Why would Reacher come to New Hope, anyway? We've seen nothing but empty fields and this is the main road from the interstate into town. Not even a barn for the past fifteen miles. No diner with a good cup of hot coffee anywhere to be found. What the hell would he be doing here?"

Gaspar shrugged. "The guy's a psycho. Nothing he's done makes any sense so far. Why should today be different?"

Kim wagged her head slowly, as if clearing the cobwebs in an enclosed space to make room for better answers, but none appeared. "What's your plan if we find him?"

Gaspar grinned, stretched, flexed his shoulders and his neck. "You worry too much. There's no designated worrier achievement medal, you know."

She'd have punched his shoulder, but her arms were too short to box across the Crown Vic's wide bench while snugged into her safety restraint. "Just because I'm the one worrying about it doesn't mean the question isn't worrisome, Chico."

He seemed briefly startled by the vibration of his personal cell phone. Gaspar patted his pockets, arched one eyebrow to accentuate his words, and asked in a playful tone, "You really think we're gonna need a plan *today*, Susie Wong?"

Kim's concern jerked several notches higher when he retrieved the phone, glanced at the caller ID, tapped the answer button, and simply said, "Hello."

Gaspar's wife was very pregnant and dealing with four kids already. Although Gaspar kept the phone close at all times, Maria had never called before. Cops' wives rarely did because receiving the wrong call at the wrong time could cause disastrous consequences. No cop's wife ever rang up out of the blue with good news; no cop receiving the call ever displayed his fear when the call came.

Kim turned aside to allow what privacy she could within the vehicle's cabin. His side of phone conversations were mostly monosyllabic anyway. Kim easily tuned him out while she considered his point.

Even if Reacher had been in New Hope yesterday,

experience told her to expect another dead end today. Perhaps she had missed something relevant. But what? She ran known facts through her head quickly.

Ten days ago, Otto and Gaspar were tasked with a routine assignment: build a file on a former military cop, applying standard background investigation techniques. The file would be used to vet him for an undisclosed classified project. Otto and Gaspar worked similar investigations as members of the FBI's Special Personnel Task Force.

The job had seemed feasibly straightforward at first. Some snafu somewhere needed ironing out.

Reacher's life was etched in bedrock government records like any other American from birth to age thirty-six, when he was honorably discharged from the Army. Up to that moment fifteen years ago, everything contained in Reacher's file was as expected. Records for birth, school, health, military, passport, driver's license, insurance, banking, and every other standard bit and byte of data existed precisely where it should have been.

The problem was that records simply stopped for Reacher at age thirty-six.

Otto and Gaspar were told to close the gap in his paper trail and bring Reacher up to date with the rest of the world. Something as simple as Reacher's death certificate would have settled the matter. Maybe it would have taken a couple of days.

Instead, everything got incredibly complicated very quickly.

Nothing about his file was normal now. Reacher's missing data traveled far beyond odd into unthinkable realms. Even when Americans were reported abducted by aliens, some secret government file somewhere existed to debunk the claim. But *nothing* for Reacher? Kim felt her head shaking, almost of its own volition. There was only one way such a thing could have happened in the real world whether Kim believed it or not; resistance was futile.

In addition, every normal resource had been declared off-limits from the outset. They were denied access to FBI resources, including personnel, computers, equipment, and databases. They had been specifically ordered not to attempt any normal channels because doing so would alert the wrong watchers. The boss delivered some line of bull to justify the straitjacket but his reasons didn't matter. Orders were orders. Rules were rules. The job was what it was.

Until someone tried to blow Gaspar into subatomic particles. After that, they'd started ignoring the boss's rules and begun creating their own.

Which was when they tried digging through back channels. Otto and Gaspar unearthed every file that might have held something, anything, connected to Reacher. Each time they came up empty—and pissed off somebody high up the food chain—they believed they were making progress. A confrontational warning delivered by Houston DEA Susan Duffy cemented their conclusions.

Whatever items remained so highly classified in Reacher's background were merely intriguing. Otto and Gaspar were comfortable with the concept of security clearances and lacking the requisite "need to know." That wasn't the problem. The total absence of those records was what worried Kim the most. Only a few highly-placed public servants had the ability to make so many routine reports disappear. And no matter how cavalierly he denied it, the gaping hole where the records should be worried Gaspar, too.

They now knew two things irrefutably and resisting the

obvious was not only futile but foolhardy. First, someone inside
government at the very highest levels had removed every piece
of documentary evidence that should have or could have existed
on Reacher for the past fifteen years. Second, Otto and Gaspar
were being used to further someone's hidden agenda.

No amount of revisiting or rearranging known facts
invalidated these conclusions. Whatever she'd missed in her
earlier analysis remained buried.

She returned her attention to the situation inside the gray
sedan. A few moments later, Gaspar signed off his phone
conversation.

Kim asked, "Everything okay at home?"

He shook his head and punched a speed-dial number on his
personal cell. Holding the phone to his ear with his shoulder, he
ran splayed fingers through his hair and expelled a long, audible
breath. "Let's not go into now, okay? We need to focus on
what's ahead."

Kim heard the robotic signals on the other end of Gaspar's
phone line. Four rings later, a man's voice answered.

Gaspar grabbed the phone and held it close to his ear,
allowing Kim to hear only one side of the conversation again.
"Alexandre?... Yeah, still on the road... Look, I need you to do
me a favor... Check on Maria this afternoon. Maybe get Denise
to stay with her a few hours and help sort things out for me...
Yeah, she'll tell you about it... Right. Turned himself in... Yeah,
it's not great... Thanks, man. I owe you... Call me when you
know more, okay? Thanks."

Gaspar ended the call and squeezed his eyes shut a few
moments. For the first time since she'd met him, Gaspar looked
old and tired and in pain. He raked his hair again, swiped his
face with his open palm, and readjusted himself on the seat. He

sucked in a deep breath followed by a long, audible exhale. Another. A third. When his breathing settled, he said nothing while he navigated the Crown Vic through the too-early winter gloom.

After a while, Kim asked, "Do you need to head back to Miami?"

He cleared his throat. Voice barely audible, he said, "Let's do what we came for while my friends get Maria settled. Then we'll see where things are."

"Why not go now? I mean, what's your confidence level we'll find anything when we get there anyway?"

Gaspar sighed, stretched, tried to get more comfortable in the seat and with his family situation, whatever it was. Kim's gut said his efforts there were futile, too.

Wearily, he lifted the edge of his mouth in a near grin before he replied, "Just following the first rule of detecting, Suzy Wong."

She liked his weak humor. Maybe that meant everything was going to be okay back at home. She hoped. "Get a better sidekick?"

He cocked his eyebrow. "I thought you didn't want to know why we're headed to New Hope."

"I don't." Trouble was, she already knew.

Early on, they figured the easiest solution to Reacher's missing records was his undocumented death. Reacher was a dangerous man who seemed to attract trouble of the fatal kind wherever he surfaced. The most likely scenario was that someone, somewhere had been bigger, faster, and more lethal than he was.

That fantasy lasted almost eight days before Kim was forced to accept that Reacher was the farthest thing from dead.

In fact, she was almost certain she'd seen him twice in the past ten days.

A giant shadow in the distance. Watching. But definitely there was a guy, and certainly matching Reacher's description.

Gaspar hadn't seen him, but he believed Kim anyway. They'd agreed. Reacher was there. He was alive and watching. For sure. At this point, he probably knew more about Otto and Gaspar than they knew about him.

Their plan had been to find people he knew before he'd vanished and move relentlessly forward to uncover the rest of his story. Maybe spotting Reacher watching them spurred this detour to New Hope; Gaspar probably figured to level the playing field by excavating more recent data. They had a chance to find Reacher now and they might never have that chance again or, at least, not for a good long while.

Which explained Gaspar's quip about the first rule of detecting: Follow the money. Money is an essential life force like air and water. Reacher's money had become relevant. Somehow, Gaspar had traced Reacher's money to New Hope. Kim knew several ways Gaspar might have exploited a weak link in the banking security system and she could imagine several more troubling sources of this intel. At some point, maybe she'd ask him. But she didn't need to do it yet.

Now they were uncomfortably close to Reacher's last known whereabouts. She wasn't exactly sure how she felt about that, but it churned her stomach like a thrashing snake. Not that her anxiety mattered. There was only one viable option. When there's only one choice, it's the right choice. Kim lived by that philosophy and followed where it led.

But they needed a plan. Just in case.

If they actually found Reacher today, Gaspar would need to

do his job and, as the lead agent on the assignment, she wanted his head back on track. Knowing what little they'd already learned about Reacher, their very lives depended on being as alert as possible.

"Is there an airport in this town?" Kim asked. She noticed Gaspar's self-satisfied smirk, which meant maybe he'd begun to compartmentalize his personal issues if he was able to tease her. She hoped.

He said, "No."

"Train station?"

"Nada."

"Bus stop?"

"Nope."

"Car rental?"

"Doubtful."

"Taxi stand?"

"Unlikely."

"So you figure he's registered at a local hotel?"

"No hotels, either."

"He hitched a ride out of town then," she said.

"A reasonable conclusion." Gaspar waited a couple of beats before he replied matter-of-factly, "Or maybe a woman invited him to stay a while."

"So your plan is what? Knock on doors looking for women of a certain age, collect Reacher and invite him out for a beer?"

She was glad to see Gaspar grin, even if he was only seeking to lighten his mood more than anything. Lighthearted was better than glum.

He said, "Not *every* woman of a certain age."

"What's your criteria?" she asked, as if his plan might be

worthwhile when she was fairly sure he was making things up as the conversation progressed.

"Only the good-looking ones."

"Models?"

"Who are single."

"Nuns?"

"And smart."

"Coeds?"

"And strong."

"Athletes?"

He waited a couple of beats for her to catch on. When she said nothing, he flashed her the look again. "And also cops."

The suggestion snatched her breath away. She felt her heart slam hard in her chest and her nostrils gulped air. She steadied her voice as well as possible. "Because?"

"Because he's a *smart* psycho. With good taste in women."

Gaspar's reasoning was sound, but she resisted. "Two women. That's hardly a reliable pattern. And you're just guessing about Duffy."

He replied, "I know why I'm here. I'm a charity case." He slapped his right thigh with his open palm. "They screwed up. Now they owe me and they're stuck with me and I can't do the job. Don't waste your time trying to make me feel better. I'm grateful for the work, but I'm expendable. I know it, they know it and you know it, too."

The possibility slamming Kim's brain felt like a caroming racquetball. She'd given no thought to why she'd been chosen. She'd been too pleased with her luck. She'd developed a detailed career plan that included achieving FBI Director status one day. She needed opportunities to prove herself and this was one such chance. Nothing more she needed to know.

When she failed to reply, Gaspar said, "Take off your rose-colored glasses, Sunshine. You think the boss picked you because you shoot straighter than the rest of us? Not to be a jerk, but get a grip."

Kim didn't argue because his facts were solid and his conclusion flawless. She had no *particular* qualifications except that she was more expendable than he was because she had no spouse and no children. Albeit for different reasons, like Gaspar, her life belonged to the FBI and that was precisely the way she liked it. She'd tried and failed at love; she had no desire to travel that road again. She was alone by choice and she intended to remain so.

Could the boss have thought she'd be Reacher bait? The idea seemed preposterous initially, but had quickly assumed potential, almost inevitability. Questions popped into her head. How could she entice Reacher to approach her? What could she offer him? What was she expected to extract in return? Why wasn't she outraged that the boss simply assumed she would sacrifice herself when the moment came?

The answer to the last question was simple. She'd sacrificed herself for the FBI before and she would do it again. The boss knew that, she knew that, and apparently Gaspar had worked it out, too.

Kim was surprised to find herself so angry. "That's your plan? We find Reacher and lure him into some compromising position and then, what? Fall on our swords?"

Gaspar shrugged. Maybe he considered anew his problem in Miami. Or maybe he was giving Kim a chance to work out a better plan now that she'd faced facts. If she dared.

CHAPTER TWO

THEY DROVE WESTWARD IN silence along the two-lane
blacktop over hilly terrain another four miles before Kim saw the
first group of modest homes lining the road on both sides. They
were widely spaced and well kept, but only a few windows were
illuminated from their interiors despite the dreary weather. Pole
buildings, barns, and other indications of rural civilization
seemed randomly placed according to no particular zoning plan
for a mile or so until the Crown Vic passed a road sign
proclaiming New Hope, Virginia's city limits. It also claimed to
have been named an All-American city a decade ago, which
seemed more than a bit ambitious for the collection of dwellings
they'd seen so far.

The county road became Valley View, widened to four
lanes, and the speed limit dropped to twenty-five miles an hour
as they approached the town. Kim felt Gaspar tap his brake to
disengage the cruise control. The big vehicle's progress
gradually slowed along the tarmac.

Nothing obstructed her line of sight. Valley View ended
ahead at a T-intersection with a landscaped ribbon of boulevard a

bit farther west. A hundred feet before the intersection with Grand Parkway, Valley View sprouted a center left turn lane and a right turn lane and Kim observed traffic signals at each turning point. The signals for turning traffic from Valley View onto Grand Parkway cycled from red to green and back, but vehicles attempting to turn north were barely moving. Traffic turning southbound and eastbound was flowing slightly better, but without regard to the cycling signals, meaning cops she couldn't see from her vantage point were most likely directing traffic.

"Can you see what's going on up there?" Kim asked, glad for the excuse to resume normal conversation.

Gaspar stretched his neck and shoulders as he slowed closer to the bottleneck. "Looks like an old crash in the right northbound lane on the boulevard, doesn't it?"

"Hard to tell from here, but I'd say an hour ago, or more." Through gaps in the traffic, Kim saw a white Ford F-150 truck with a cap on the bed stopped on Grand Parkway about thirty feet north of the intersection.

The Crown Vic progressed haltingly along Valley View with no discernible rhythm to its forward movement. After a bit, Gaspar said, "There's a blue Toyota Prius's front end wedged under the truck's back bumper. That Prius is crunched up like it hit a brick wall at twenty-five miles an hour, but the truck looks undamaged."

"I'm counting maybe seven sets of flashing lights. No sirens, so yeah, they've probably been there a while. Blue, red, and white, but no yellow," Kim said.

Gaspar groused, leaned his head back and closed his eyes. "One day they're going to standardize emergency vehicle lighting in this country."

"Maybe. But right now, I'd say an ambulance is standing by,

injuries were already dealt with, and locals are directing traffic and documenting the scene. But they've got no tow trucks to move the damaged vehicles out of the way, so they've got a snarl." Kim's mind appreciated the exercise of figuring out a simple, solvable puzzle for a change. Even though the solution was far from ideal. A tie-up at an intersection like this could take hours to resolve and she wasn't excited about spending the night in New Hope, Virginia.

"Seems like a lot of responders for a routine rear-end collision," Gaspar said without looking. "So you're probably right about the injuries."

Traffic continued to move slowly around the crash site. From time to time, Gaspar lifted his foot off the brake and allowed the Crown Vic to inch ahead. When they were close enough, Kim saw two uniformed police officers standing in the biting wind directing traffic, which was surprisingly heavy. They hadn't seen a single vehicle on the road in the hour before they reached the city limits. She guessed the bulk of New Hope's population must lie along Grand Boulevard. Or maybe this was rush hour.

There wasn't much to look at until they were allowed to make their own right turn and travel slowly past the crash site, craning their necks to watch the show along with the other gawkers.

Kim saw a woman, clothes bloody, shivering under a too-small blanket, perhaps awaiting an ambulance. A towheaded boy, maybe about four years old and wearing a sweater and corduroy jeans stood a short distance away. Oddly for a crash victim, if he was one, the boy seemed to be chatting amiably with a uniformed policewoman. But it was the oversized mound Kim saw on the pavement covered by another dark blanket that caught her attention as Gaspar threaded the needle to move them beyond the scene.

"Pull over on the right," Kim said.

"Are you sure you want to do that? Even if Reacher's lying dead under there, we're supposed to be keeping a low profile, don't forget."

She didn't argue. Fifty feet from the official vehicles, Gaspar pulled off and parked on the wide gravel shoulder. They stepped out of the Crown Vic and into the stinging wind. The air smelled heavy with loam and exhaust. Humidity soaked her skin like a cold cloud bath.

"Aren't you Latin lovers supposed to be chivalrous? Why don't you ever have a coat to offer me?" Kim teased, shivering from nerves as well as cold as they trudged through damp earth toward the body.

"November's always great beach weather in Miami and I don't own a coat." Gaspar had stuffed his hands in his trouser pockets after turning up his Banana Republic suit collar. "You're a liberated female from Detroit. What's your excuse?"

Kim wondered that herself. She made a mental note to stop at the first affordable department store. Surely somewhere in this town she might be able to find a coat to fit her, even if she had to shop in the girls' department.

Gaspar didn't dawdle even though his leg had to be cramped after all the driving. Kim struggled to keep up with his long strides. She didn't know the full extent of his injuries and he'd made it clear she wasn't going to find out more from him. Snooping into his background seemed disloyal; she'd wait until he trusted her enough to explain. He limped a little, but as they continued along he seemed to walk it out somehow.

First responders handled the chaotic scene appropriately,

Kim noticed. Maybe this was a small town in the middle of nowhere, but officials performed as if they'd been well trained. Emergent needs had been attended to. Now they were processing the crime scene and handling traffic. No one seemed interested in the blanket or the body that lay beneath.

When Otto and Gaspar approached, a plain-clothes official standing off to the side noticed. He was a slim man, maybe forty-five or fifty, graying chestnut hair and thick black brows. He didn't ask if they knew the parties involved in the crash, but his tone was friendly when he said, "I'm afraid you folks are going to have to return to your car."

Gaspar waited for Otto to take the lead. Partly because stopping was her idea, but leading was also her job. She pulled out her badge wallet and held it in her left hand as she extended her right to shake, counting on the local guy to return her gesture automatically, which he did.

"Looks like you have your hands full here," Kim said, friendly too, slipping her badge back into her pocket. Now he'd have to request it if he wanted a closer look. Most times, they didn't. All cops knew an FBI shield at a glance. Gaspar didn't offer a glimpse of his. All cops knew FBI agents traveled in pairs.

"Chief Paul Brady, New Hope PD," he said, a voice that might sing tenor in the church choir. "You must have been diverted here, huh? Sorry to interrupt your work, but thanks for coming so quickly. Rest of your team on the way?"

Brady's words jolted her spine like a Taser strike. Why would a local chief call the FBI on a traffic fatality? Sure, headquarters was only a couple of hours away, but the FBI's jurisdiction didn't include traffic crashes under normal circumstances.

Kim injected her tone with cooperative officiousness. "Why'd you call us?"

Chief Brady said, "I didn't initially. Witnesses said carjacking. Never been common around here and I hadn't heard the term for at least a decade."

Carjacking wasn't FBI jurisdiction, either, but Kim didn't say so. She figured Brady for a guy who had to tell a story in his own way and his own time. "Uh, huh."

Brady stuck his paws inside his jacket pockets. "The thing kinda snowballed. First caller reported a rear end collision. I sent a patrol unit out here to process that. A minute or two later, second caller said road rage. Said a huge guy got out of the truck with a shotgun. I quick dispatched another unit. Third caller said the truck driver bashed the Prius's window with the shotgun butt, dragged the woman out of the Prius and beat her with the gun like it was a club." Brady wagged his head back and forth as if he couldn't believe road rage would lead to such savagery, even though he knew it had. "When my officers arrived on the scene, they found the woman battered, the guy dead on the ground, and the boy screaming inside the car. That's when I grabbed my coat and dashed over here."

Gaspar shivered in the cold dampness, scowling as Brady's tale unfolded too slowly. Her partner wasn't interested in explaining things to annoyed colleagues arriving any moment. Kim knew because she felt the same way.

But she *needed* to see the big guy under that blanket. She didn't actually believe Reacher was lying under there. Not really. She didn't believe he'd been in New Hope at all. Not yesterday or ever. But one quick look would settle it and she was ten feet away and she wasn't leaving until she knew for sure.

Gaspar prodded Brady to get to the relevant facts supporting

FBI jurisdiction. "Domestic terrorists? Contraband in the car? She killed him with an illegal weapon? Guy's a Native American?"

Brady's scowl matched Gaspar's now as the alpha males squared off. Kim intervened to avoid a stalemate, which would be worse than a skirmish at the moment. "You'd know everybody in town, Chief. Who are these folks?"

Maybe Brady didn't want a skirmish, either. "Well, see, that's the thing. The Prius is a rental from West Virginia. The F-150 is a Maryland rental. We ran the plates. Both were picked up a week ago using a corporate credit card. We're running that down now, but we keep hitting dead ends on the paper trail."

"No ID on the deceased?"

"None."

"The woman?"

"Says her name is Jill Hill, but she has no ID, either."

"What about the boy?" Gaspar asked. "He looks like a little man who knows his name and address to me."

"He is all of that," Chief Brady's mouth lifted in a slight grin. "Cute kid. Charmed every one of us. He says his name is Brook and he's asking if the giant went to climb the beanstalk."

CHAPTER THREE

KIM NODDED AND TOOK a deep breath. "Let's go see what you've got before any more daylight gets away from us."

She began walking toward the body, leaving chief Brady and Gaspar no choice but to follow. The F-150 and the Prius were almost bonded together at the crumple, meaning they had to walk around. Kim made her way through small openings between official vehicles attempting to block the crime scene from gawkers. Various personnel were milling around while they waited for the FBI to take over. Kim had no intention of doing so. Her immediate plan was to confirm that Reacher was lying dead under the blanket. Or not.

Depending on how this went, Kim might or might not want to leave. Less than a minute later Otto and Gaspar stood beside the hulking mound. Her body hummed as if she were electrically connected to a power source. This could be him. The assignment would be over. She wasn't sure how she felt about that; nor did her feelings matter. It was what it was.

Gaspar asked a paramedic to remove the cover.

When they lifted the blanket, Kim required only the briefest glance to settle her questions. She glanced at Gaspar. He nodded. His face was a mess. His nose was pulped and his cheekbones smashed. Hair was fair and long, hung over his ears and below his collar. He had the thick neck and heavy shoulders of a bodybuilder. His thighs bulged inside indigo jeans. He wore heavy work boots on his feet. The shotgun remained clutched in his right hand. Dead eyes stared at nothing. His forehead was red and swollen and might yet bruise, even though his heart had finally ceased pumping not long after he cracked his skull open on the pavement's edge. Bad luck, falling just there, where frost had heaved the pavement to a sharp edge harder than the guy's head.

No doubt he seemed like a giant to the boy. He was about 6'2" tall, maybe 220 pounds. The man really was huge. But not big enough to be Jack Reacher.

While she dealt with the adults, Gaspar approached the remaining eyewitness. Kim pulled out her smart phone and snapped a few photos before she asked the paramedics to replace the blanket. She noticed the deepening dusk and glanced at her Seiko to check the time. Soon, the official FBI team would arrive. She hoped they were bringing sufficient lighting. In another thirty minutes, they'd be working with only insufficient ambient light to process the scene.

She turned her attention next to the woman. Jill Hill. The name sounded silly enough to be real, but Kim figured it was more likely made up on the spur of the moment when someone asked and Jill wasn't prepared with a better lie. Because she had the phone out already, she snapped a few pictures of Ms. Hill, too.

Ms. Hill shivered under the blanket the paramedic had wrapped around her. Her blonde hair was matted with blood, probably from a scalp laceration. Scalp wounds bled like faucets. An effort had been made to wipe the blood from her battered, swollen face, but her broken nose was going to require surgery. Maybe her cheekbones were broken, too. It was hard to say given the lighting conditions. When she watched Kim, her pupils were uneven and nonreactive.

Kim was no doctor, but like all FBI agents she'd had extensive emergency first aid training. And what she saw alarmed her. She waved Chief Brady over and reported quietly, "She needs to be transported now."

Brady said, "We didn't think she was emergent. We were waiting for FBI to make the call."

Instead of asking why again, Kim said, "Now's the time." She understood the protocols for concurrent FBI jurisdiction. But if Jill Hill died for killing this man, Kim wanted that to be a decision made by the justice system and not the result when law enforcement failed to provide treatment.

Gaspar had crouched low, eye-to-eye with the boy, engaged in lively conversation. He was an adorable child who looked maybe a little familiar. Blonde curls, dancing blue eyes, sweetly cherubic cheeks, and a bubbly smile accentuated by a heart-shaped full mouth. Kim noticed only one odd note: Whatever happened here seemed not to have troubled him overmuch.

Kim tapped Gaspar on the shoulder. He looked up and she tilted her head toward the Crown Vic. He nodded agreement. They'd been here too long. The unmistakable whap-whap-whap of a helicopter, no doubt bringing the FBI agents actually assigned to the case, grew louder. If they hurried, they could be gone before the official team disembarked.

The boy glanced at Kim and popped up wearing a drooling grin. "I'm Brook! You're tall as me!" he said, clearly delighted to find at least one adult occupying space near his vertical dimension.

Kim felt her back stiffen, raised to her full 4'11" height and straightened her shoulders before she teased, "In your dreams, Bucko!"

He giggled as if this was the funniest thing any adult had said to him today. Which, sadly, it might have been. He offered her a high five. She slapped palms with him, somewhat chagrined to realize that his hand was not so much smaller than hers.

Gaspar had struggled out of his crouch. "We've gotta go, buddy. I had fun talking to you."

Young Brook shook hands solemnly with each of them. Then he giggled his glorious laugh and waved while in a singsong voice he said, "Ta-ta! See you in the funny pages!"

"You bet," Kim replied. *Where have I heard that phrase delivered just like that before?*

They hastened toward the Crown Vic, not only because of the cold, but because the whapping chopper blades had stopped.

Chief Brady stepped into their path before they reached the Crown Vic. "We sent a couple of cars to collect your team. They should be here shortly. We'll let you get right to it. Meet up later in my office?"

"That works," Kim said. "But you never told me why you called the FBI in the first place."

Briefly, Brady's brows joined over the bridge of his nose in puzzlement before enlightenment struck. "Why did we know about the kidnapping, you mean?"

Kidnapping?

"We recognized the kid from the classified BOLO." Brady

chuckled like a proud papa. "He looks exactly like his grandfather, don't you think? What a charmer. This kid is likely to be president instead of vice president when he grows up, huh? He's already got the wave and the farewell line down pat."

CHAPTER FOUR

KIM FELT ABOUT TWO beats behind while she made the connection. Of course, the boy was former Vice President Brook Armstrong's grandson. That's why his farewell words seemed so familiar. Otto and Gaspar had been living so far under the radar, they hadn't even known about the kidnapping. Agencies would have been advised officially, but a media blackout would have been imposed until sometime later as a matter of national security. Kids of politicians were protected from the bright world spotlight. But FBI agents would have known.

Gaspar must have been similarly behind the curve because he didn't immediately jump in, either. Half a moment later, they completely lost their opportunity to leave undetected.

Chief Brady's gaze moved and fixed at a point beyond. "Here's your team now," he said.

Otto and Gaspar heard the lead agent speak behind them as she approached and moved into their line of sight. "Susan Duffy. Chief Brady?"

Brady nodded and shook hands and delivered a succinct summary, "Agent Otto here has already sent one injured woman to the hospital. One dead. And the boy is with one of my officers."

Perhaps Duffy decided to be discreet for the moment. She said, "Otto and Gaspar can catch me up, Chief. My team will come with you to the crash site. There's another chopper and team on the way to collect the child. I'll be right there."

When Brady and the other agents moved out of earshot, Duffy's congeniality disappeared. Her tone was as cold as the frigid wind. "Why are you here?"

Kim might have attempted conciliation if she hadn't felt like a complete fool. She hated being ignorant of a major alert for the entire national security team. And Duffy knew too much about Otto and Gaspar already. Belligerence was called for. "Same reason you are. Reacher. Where is he?"

Duffy didn't flinch. "You're confused, Agent Otto. Building the Reacher file is your assignment, not mine."

Gaspar intervened. "You can do better than that. Maybe this kidnapping isn't our case, but it's not yours either, is it? You didn't tell Grady you're BATF, so he wasn't expecting you. Which means Reacher must have called you and that's why *you're* here. What are you worried about?"

Duffy seemed to consider things for a moment or two longer than necessary. Probably running the possible scenarios through her mind, deciding how much to reveal, what to conceal. Kim recognized the signs.

Duffy said, "Our team was deployed to assist with apprehension of kidnapping suspects and the continuing commission of federal crimes."

She'd chosen the option Kim would have selected and that was a comfort because it made Duffy predictable, which was the best thing an adversary could be. Kim would bet a month's salary Duffy's answer wasn't true, but it was vague enough. The kind of thing Duffy could maintain long enough to do whatever it was she'd come here to accomplish.

Gaspar raised his right eyebrow in response.

Duffy bluffed again, probably because they were in no position to challenge her bluff. "You can check with my superiors if you like before you brief me on exactly why *you're* here. I'll wait."

Gaspar shrugged like a man who's played more than one hand of poker, too. "We were in process of our assignment when we approached what we thought was a traffic crash with bodily injury. We stopped to help. Now that you're here and in charge, we'll head out unless there's something we can do for you?"

Before Duffy had a chance to reply, an officer from Brady's team walked up, "Agent Duffy? The medical examiner wants to see you before they transport the body. Please come this way." Duffy simply followed; Otto and Gaspar tagged along.

The medical examiner was standing beside the covered body when they approached. "We've followed protocols, Agent Duffy. Is there anything special you want me to check before I go?"

"Identifying marks? Scars? Anything?" she asked, as if she thought there might be. Kim realized Duffy hadn't seen the body. Yet, she didn't seem to be thinking Reacher had found his match at long last and finally lost. She didn't seem worried at all.

"Unfortunately, no," the doctor said. "I've taken extra cheek swabs for DNA in case you have anything to compare at some point. But there is something I wanted to show you."

The medical examiner knelt down beside the body. Duffy tensed slightly and Kim wondered why; she already knew the dead man wasn't Reacher. Did Duffy know who the guy was?

He removed the blanket. He turned the burly man's head to the side exposing his ruined skull. "Cause of death appears to be blunt trauma to the skull caused by hitting the broken concrete. The curious thing is how his head landed here with sufficient force to cause this much damage."

"He'd fall pretty hard, wouldn't he?"

The doctor wagged his head. "I can show you the computer models later, but the short answer is that's unlikely."

Gaspar asked, "Meaning what?"

"Meaning he was pushed and pushed hard."

Kim felt what was coming in the same way she'd feel vibrations on a train track before the train appeared. Maybe Duffy felt it, too.

The doctor gestured toward the burly man's forehead. "See the redness and swelling here? If he'd lived, he'd have a hell of a bruise tomorrow. He was hit with considerable force and weight, which knocked him backwards at significant velocity. When he hit the concrete the blow was much stronger than a simple slip or push and fall."

Duffy's face was a mask of objectivity. But Kim wanted firm, unshakable answers. "Could the woman have hit him hard enough to cause this?"

"I don't know for sure, but in my opinion, no. She's been described to me as slight and five feet, four inches tall. That makes the leverage wrong. I doubt she could have wielded any weapon with sufficient force to knock this guy down in this way, particularly in her weakened condition after he had already attacked her." He wagged his head again, "I don't see how any normal-sized woman could have done it."

"So you're saying someone else killed this guy?" Kim asked, to be clear.

"That's how it looks," he said.

"What knocked him down?" Gaspar asked.

"Hard to say. Something unexpected, because the deceased didn't see it coming and duck away. Something hard, heavy, strong. Not that shotgun we found lying there, for sure."

Duffy interrupted, "Thank you, doctor. Call me from the hospital after you've seen the woman, please." She handed him her business card. Then she turned to face Kim. "Let's get a cup of coffee. It's freezing out here."

Otto and Gaspar walked behind Duffy the short distance back to the Crown Vic. As Duffy had foretold, a second, larger helicopter approached from the east, moving fast, rotors progressively louder, almost within range. Conversational tones became impossible.

Once all three were seated inside the car, Kim turned toward the back seat; Duffy's gaze met Gaspar's in the rear view mirror. She said, "You're looking thoughtful."

Gaspar started the engine and flipped on the heat before he replied, "Just thinking that what little Brook said to me makes a lot more sense now."

"What'd he say?" Kim asked, still watching Duffy. *What was she thinking?*

Gaspar said, "Brook wanted to know why the giant killed the bad man."

Duffy's scowl consumed her facial features like a plaster mask. "You've jumped to the wrong conclusions again. We need to talk before you get too far off the rails, which wouldn't be a good thing for any of us."

Still, Kim examined Duffy's reaction carefully, challenged. "You're saying Reacher didn't kill that guy?"

Duffy's sigh was barely audible over the rotors' noise. "It's not what you think, Otto."

Kim wagged her head with vigor. "Nothing about Reacher ever is." Neither Duffy nor Gaspar heard.

Gaspar's near-shout barely traveled across the increasing cacophony. "Why don't you enlighten us?"

Duffy projected loudly, "That's my plan. There's a diner on Grand Boulevard about a mile past the police station. Head north. I'll tell you where to turn."

Gaspar pulled the big car onto the northbound lane and joined the spotty traffic traveling now at normal speeds. New Hope was a tidy town populated with Disney-like storefronts and gaslights and lined with flower boxes still sporting fall mums in yellow hues. The sidewalks were swept clean. The only thing missing were shoppers, but given the weather and the hour and the excitement back at the intersection, an absence of pedestrians was not surprising.

Three miles beyond the crime scene stood a freestanding red brick building with white Doric columns and an impressive double door. Once, it might have been a bank. Now, The New Hope Family Diner advertised breakfast all day. Duffy said, "Park in the side lot. There's an entrance there."

Also in the side lot were a dozen vehicles of various makes and models. At the end of the row, Kim noticed a standard issue government black SUV with dark tinted windows all around the back. The driver was clean cut, well-groomed, and infinitely patient.

Duffy led the way inside the diner and chose a booth in the back away from the other patrons. Duffy sat with her back to the exit, leaving Kim and Gaspar the best position choice. *Surprising,* Kim thought, as she and Gaspar sat facing the door.

After the waitress had taken their orders and delivered the coffee, Duffy said, "You've been out of the loop on this situation so let me fill you in first. The Vice President's daughter and her husband are divorcing. The divorce is contentious and not going well for her."

Kim had heard the rumors. Sally Armstrong had been a wild child when her father was one heartbeat away from leading the free world. Substance abuse was alleged, but never admitted. Marriage hadn't tamed her.

Gaspar watched Duffy closely while drinking his coffee, but he asked no questions, which was odd for him. His behavior had been erratic since his wife called earlier. Kim continued to worry about his Miami issues, but she could only handle one major problem at a time.

"Go on," Kim said.

Duffy said, "Six days ago, young Brook Armstrong III was kidnapped from his home in Arlington by his nanny, Jillian Timmer, and an unidentified man."

"Otherwise known as 'Jill Hill' and the dead truck driver I suppose," Kim said.

Duffy nodded. "Jillian had disabled the surveillance cameras, but she wasn't aware of additional surveillance inside and outside the Armstrong house. As a result, the Vice President's team knew fairly quickly that the two had abducted the boy. The kidnapping was well planned and well executed."

Gaspar wiped his hand across his face and made a strange, almost moaning noise. His voice filled with anger and accusation. "Meaning Jillian executed the kidnapping with the cooperation of one of Brook's parents, and you were one of the people supposed to keep that from happening, and then the team lost visual contact before they could be apprehended, right?"

Duffy's annoyance flashed, but she tamped down her temper. The effort cost her. "After that, we worked around the clock to find the boy. None of us has slept more than four hours in the past six days. We expected a ransom demand, but it never came."

Kim quickly put the timeline together in her head. "So you were working the case three days ago, when we saw you in DC."

Pieces of the puzzle were clicking into place, but what did the full picture look like?

Duffy had lowered her gaze and drank a few sips of black coffee before she continued. "We got a lucky break today. I received an anonymous tip—"

Gaspar's fist pounded the table, nostrils flared, a deep flush rose from his collar to his hairline. "Seriously? You expect me to believe *that*?"

A few diners glanced toward their table, maybe alarmed, maybe curious about the fuss. Duffy cleared her throat and continued as if he'd never spoken. "I received an anonymous tip a few hours ago. Brook was seen riding in a vehicle involved in an insignificant rear end collision here in New Hope. While we put everything in place to pick him up here, the truck driver got out of hand. You arrived before we did."

"What a load of crap," Gaspar said, angrier than Kim had seen him in their brief time as partners. Was he angry because of Duffy's lies? Or was it something else?

Duffy's eyes flashed anger now, too. But she remained seated. She drank coffee and, like Kim, waited for Gaspar to settle down. When he did, she handed them a hand-held video device.

"Press the play button," she said.

CHAPTER FIVE

OTTO AND GASPAR WATCHED the scene unfold on Duffy's video like a silent movie. The video was obviously spliced from images captured by several sources. The early segments were recorded by drones without soundtrack and maybe some kind of interior vehicle cameras. Later portions contained some sound and a bit of dialogue, indicating they were recorded by traffic cams and maybe other sources. The images were good enough. Clear enough to confirm some things. Not clear enough for others.

The sign advising sixteen miles to New Hope's city limits was four miles back on the road before the video's start. The hitchhiker was hunched into his jacket like cold and damp and heavy November air chilled his bones even as he trudged westward along the road's uneven shoulder at a warming clip. Stinging wind assaulted his face so he kept his head down.

Nothing to see, anyway. The bleak landscape was less welcoming than any Kim had traveled before, which was quite a feat. He probably felt the same.

Experience must have told him to keep moving until, maybe,

the right vehicle came along. A farmer or trucker could have offered him a ride; maybe that's how he reached this point. Otherwise, he'd walk another four hours before he found hot coffee and a decent diner and, if he could muster a little luck, a warm bed for the night.

He'd made such trips before and Kim figured he expected more long walks down empty roads toward new towns in his future.

But Kim recognized him immediately because she'd seen him twice before. She recognized his clothes, too. The same heavy work boots probably kept his feet warm enough, dry enough. The brown leather jacket's collar was turned up and his hair covered his ears, but a cap and gloves would have improved things, weather-wise. Indigo jeans and a work shirt surely weren't sufficient. She wondered why he didn't wear something warmer, at the very least.

"That's Reacher, isn't it?" Kim asked. A test for Duffy. How far could she be trusted?

Duffy replied, "Can't see the face."

Which wasn't exactly true, but Kim figured Duffy knew the value of plausible deniability, too, and maybe Duffy's response was better than an affirmation for now.

"Why was he there?" Kim asked.

"I'm not a mind reader," Duffy said, a little huffily this time.

So she doesn't know why. And she's pissed off about it. Interesting.

Reacher looked less like a guy down on his luck and more like a threat, but there was nothing he could do about his travel costume then, even if he'd cared about fashion, which he probably didn't.

Kim wondered aloud, "Why was he headed to New Hope along that lonely road this afternoon? He was already here yesterday. Where did he go and why was he coming back?"

No one answered. Maybe someday, Kim would have the chance to ask him. She felt her stomach churn at the thought and controlled it by turning her attention back to the video.

Heavy clouds threatened snow to blanket the countryside again before nightfall. He could have slept outside. He'd done it many times before when he was in the army. But maybe he had a plan for a room in New Hope, although everything she knew about him said he wasn't much of an advance planner.

"There," Gaspar said, pointing with his chin, one eyebrow raised. "See it?"

She did. He'd picked his head up. His stride hesitated briefly.

Kim said, "He heard the car approaching when it was far behind him. Good ears."

"He's got years of training and sharp reflexes. And it was probably just quiet enough out there. The engine would've sounded small and weak and foreign. You can almost see him thinking it through, knowing he'd have trouble scrunching his six-foot, five-inch frame into the passenger seat."

Or maybe he was expecting the Prius all along because Duffy told him what car Jillian was driving, Kim thought. *Maybe that's why he was there to start with.*

Gaspar said, "Alternative rides weren't thick on the ground. He probably figured nothing more suitable was likely to pass before nightfall."

A few moments later, Reacher had turned to face oncoming traffic and stuck out his right thumb, walking slowly backward, waiting. Kim recalled too clearly the biting wind that scraped her corneas. Must have been the same for him and caused his eyes to water, too.

He'd have watched through watery haze while the blue vehicle steadily narrowed the distance between them without slowing. Some optical trick might've made the car seem smaller as it came closer, which made no sense at all, but Kim had experienced that, too.

He blinked until his vision cleared, maybe. He saw a female at the wheel, alone in the Prius. Blonde hair. Nice face. Gorgeous eyes. Dark sweater. Maybe mid-thirties. Kim was shocked by Jillian's face. The face Kim saw after Jillian was viciously attacked by the truck driver, wasn't recognizable as this same woman.

Jillian glanced toward Reacher as she passed without slowing. Now, he blinked the water out of his eyes and closed his lids briefly.

"He couldn't have been surprised," Kim said. "What woman in her right mind would pick up a guy looking like him?"

Gaspar replied. "No woman should pick up *any* hitchhiker, Sunshine. Not even you. And I don't care how good a marksman you are."

Kim didn't bother to defend against his challenge because she agreed with him on principle. But if Jillian had followed her first instincts and simply kept going, she'd be dead now. Maybe she'd known that. Maybe she knew that violence is a process, not an event.

After the Prius passed, Reacher turned to face westward again and resumed trudging, his head down against the frigid wind once more.

Less than five minutes later, he must've heard the puny engine's unmistakable whine again. He glanced up and saw the same driver behind the wheel. Maybe he wondered why she'd changed her mind. What did he think? Probably some misguided act of Christian charity or something?

The car passed him again, made a U-turn, returned and pulled up alongside. Jillian lowered the passenger side window and he bent over to speak to her. It was then he would have seen Brook belted into a booster seat on the passenger side. Young Brook's head was barely as high as the window's edge.

"What's going through his head now?" Kim asked, as if she was talking to herself.

"He's thinking she's either very brave or very foolish," Gaspar said. "What's she thinking?"

"Maybe she figured the boy would provide a level of security. She couldn't possibly have known whether he would hurt her or the boy, right? Was she stupid? Crazy? Both?"

Gaspar shrugged. "To him, her motives didn't matter. Hers was the only car he'd seen in the past hour and he was cold and tired and hungry. The only thing that mattered to him at the moment was getting somewhere to bunk in for the night rather than sleeping outside in the snow."

The boy grinned. His eyelids seemed heavy. A bit of drool dampened the side of his smile. Blue eyes widened when Reacher doubled over to stick his head in the window.

The boy said something. Reacher smiled at him, tried to look less menacing. No success.

Jillian shouted from the driver seat against the wind rushing in around him through the open window. Maybe she asked where he was going or maybe she just suggested he hop in. Impossible to tell from the silent video.

He said something. Pointed toward the town twelve miles ahead. He waited and she watched him a couple of moments, trying to decide, probably. Maybe he was mildly curious about her next move. If a normal man had had any reasonable option, he might have allowed her to keep driving, collecting nothing but a story to tell her girlfriends about the hulking, menacing hitchhiker who'd flagged her down on the way into town.

He reached back and opened the passenger door quickly, maybe worried she'd come to her senses and speed away. He folded himself into the back seat awkwardly; his bulk barely allowed him to close the door.

The boy tried to turn around and look at him, but the seatbelt held him firmly in the federally certified and approved safety restraint system. Kim was glad the restraints worked because he should have been in the back seat. Brook wiggled a little bit before he gave up and asked his questions without eye contact.

Kim could see the child's lips moving, but she couldn't hear his words. "What did he ask about, do you know?"

Gaspar grinned. "He told me the whole thing, blow by blow. He wanted to know if Mr. Giant had a beanstalk they could climb. But it was a short conversation. Long on questions from young Brook and short on answers from the giant."

Jillian reached over and ruffled the boy's curls in a gesture as old as motherhood itself. She maybe asked him to be quiet and play with his toys. He seemed to do that and Kim saw no signs of unhappiness from either the woman or the boy. Had Reacher assumed Jillian was Brook's mother? A reasonable, if incorrect, assumption.

Jillian glanced into her rearview mirror to meet his gaze and spoke to him. Whatever he replied satisfied her because she turned her attention back to driving and soon had the car moving steadily westward again.

"What did she say to him?" Kim asked.

Duffy said, "I don't know. Maybe she'll be able to tell us when we have a chance to question her."

Reacher closed his eyes and dropped his chin to his chest. Apparently, he wasn't in the mood for conversation. After a few contortions, he slouched further down onto the backseat.

"Is he sleeping?" Kim asked aloud.

"I would be," Gaspar replied.

Twenty-one minutes later the car had stopped at the intersection of Valley View and Grand Parkway, waiting for the traffic signal. The boy must have dropped something; Jillian seemed to be searching on the floor or maybe between the seats.

The traffic light changed to green, allowing westbound traffic to proceed. But the little car didn't move immediately.

Gaspar said, "This would have been the point where witnesses reported the first long horn blast from the F-150 immediately behind her car. Another long one, then two shorter blasts followed, Brady said."

"We've got spotty sound from here on out," Duffy said. She reached over to turn up the volume.

On the video, Jillian stopped searching for the toy and sat up abruptly. She slid the transmission into gear. Kim could see her lips moving as she spoke silently. Maybe she said, "Okay, okay, okay. Keep your shirt on. We're going." Or something like that.

Jillian pulled the vehicle through the intersection making a right turn and curving narrowly moving into the far right lane, allowing the angry truck driver plenty of room to pass. Kim heard his revved engine amid traffic sounds from other cars in the intersection. Jillian's Prius floated side to side in the truck's wash as it sped past.

And that should have been the end of it. In a more civilized age, it would have been. But not this day. Because whether

Jillian knew it or not, violence is still a process, not an event, and the day wasn't finished yet.

Instead, Jillian continued her steady stream of nervous chatter, but whatever she said inside the car was inaudible through the available surveillance microphones and the image wasn't the right angle for lip reading.

But the horns, the lost toy, Jillian's agitation, and probably a hundred other things altogether flipped a switch of some sort and the boy began to squall while still safely belted into his car seat.

Jillian glanced over, maybe to comfort the child. In the split second she was distracted, she didn't see the F-150 stop abruptly in front of her and the Prius slammed into what must have felt like hitting a brick building.

From the back seat, her passenger had no warning and no opportunity to brace himself. The impact threw him onto the floor in a jumble of boots and knees and elbows. Maybe his head took a resounding whack against the padded front seat.

Brook cried harder and Jillian panicked, yelling now, probably near hysteria, which fed the boy's squalling and the cacophony inside the car must have reached decibels assaulting all ears.

The truck driver moved swiftly from inside the F-150's cab to standing beside the Prius holding his shotgun by the barrel like a club or a baseball bat.

Kim and Gaspar watched Reacher struggle to extricate himself from his tortured position in the foot well. When the truck driver smashed Jillian's window, Reacher must have heard the sound of breaking glass and felt the rush of cold air into the cabin.

Jillian screamed and the boy continued screeching and while Reacher was still struggling to get up off the floor. The truck driver's angry tenor shouted, "What the hell is wrong with you, bitch?"

That was the point where the truck driver opened Jillian's door and hauled her out and threw her hard against the car.

Gaspar pressed the pause button on the playback to give them a moment Reacher didn't have at the time to think through the situation.

CHAPTER SIX

BY THE TIME REACHER was able to assess the situation, chaos reigned. The Prius's front end had smashed into the rear of the oversized F-150 and crunched like an accordion. The burly driver, outraged, unrelenting, held Jillian by the arm and shook her, screaming angry words Reacher, still in the back seat, couldn't quite hear, either. The boy continued his hysteria in the front seat and the little car's horn, which had sounded constantly since the collision, blared as if its battery might last forever.

The truck driver raised the shotgun and brought the butt down on Jillian's shoulder hard enough to knock her out of his grasp and drop her to the pavement.

In a flash, Reacher propelled from the back seat, over the wrinkled car hood, and when the burly guy raised his shotgun club again, Reacher grabbed the gun barrel, stopping the swing at the top of his arc and causing the burly guy's weight to shift and pivot on his left foot.

Surprise caught the burly guy off guard for a moment, but a moment was all Reacher needed. Briefly, their eyes met and the truck driver's bulged as if he was being squeezed by a bullwhip around the stomach.

That was when the burly driver made his final mistake. He faced Reacher full on and snarled a threat that seemed to faze Reacher not at all.

Out of the blue, Reacher head-butted him full in the face. Came off his back foot, thrust up the legs and whipped his head forward and smashed it into the guy's nose, like hitting him in the face with a bowling ball.

His legs crumpled and he hit the floor like a puppet with the strings cut.

And his head cracked on the concrete's jagged edge.

When the truck driver went down and stayed down, Reacher moved swiftly to Jillian's side. He helped her to her feet, steadied her inside the Prius, then knelt to talk with her, watching her face carefully, maybe looking for the non-reactive pupils Kim saw hours later. They exchanged a few words the microphones didn't catch, but it seemed like a brief and gentle disagreement.

Jillian waved toward the moving traffic. A few vehicles had slowed and some had stopped. A man held a cell phone to his ear. A woman dressed in nurse's garb approached to help. Jillian glanced at Reacher once more and a long look communicating something unspoken passed between them.

More cars slowed, stopped, and people came to help.

Reacher stood, turned, and walked northward along Grand Boulevard's gravel shoulder. In the final moments of the video, his image was grainy, indistinct. Perhaps another drone camera's capture or maybe Duffy had cut the sound.

Reacher seemed to have a cell phone held to his ear. Then he dropped it onto the pavement and crushed it with the heel of his boot before he turned, stuck out his thumb, and waited for a ride.

The video ended. Silence reigned while the three agents mulled things over.

Duffy said, "I'm going to the restroom. I'll be right back." She picked up the video player and left the table.

Gaspar said, "I have to call Maria." He left the table, too, and Kim heard, "Alexandre? How is she?" before he moved through the front door of The New Hope Family Diner in search of a better signal.

CHAPTER SEVEN

KIM REMAINED SEATED, TRYING to make sense of the puzzle picture and Reacher's jumbled profile as Duffy's video destroyed the working hypothesis she'd formed in her head.

Several things that had been mysteries a few hours ago were now solved. Duffy had done Reacher a favor three days ago when she warned Otto and Gaspar to stop digging for Reacher's records. Reacher probably came to New Hope to return that favor.

He figured somehow that Jillian Timmer and Brook Armstrong were hiding here. Reacher discovered or deduced a connection between Jillian and New Hope, even if Duffy didn't know what it was yet. Maybe she or Kim would find the connection, but it didn't really matter now that the kidnapping was resolved and Reacher had obviously moved on.

Maybe Reacher had planned to kill the truck driver and maybe not. Either way would no doubt have been fine with Reacher.

The confounding point was his motivation. Was it possible

that all he wanted was to release Jillian from the man's hold and help Duffy return Brook to his family?

Gaspar returned to the table, smiling a little, Kim thought. "Maria doing better?"

"She's got a ways to go, but thank God for Alexandre and Denise. They're staying with her, helping with the kids until I can get back. I'll tell you about it later. Where's Duffy?"

Kim looked out into the parking lot and noticed that the black SUV with the tinted windows and government plates was gone.

THE END

JACK

IN THE
GREEN

*Thank you to some of the best readers in the world:
Natalie Chernow, Angie Shaw (Noah Daniel),
Dan Chillman (Danimal), Lynette Bartos (Derek Bartos),
Teresa Burgess (Trista Blanke) for participating in our
character naming giveaways which make this book
a bit more personal and fun for all of us.*

*Perpetually, for Lee Child,
with unrelenting gratitude.*

CAST OF PRIMARY CHARACTERS

Kim L. Otto
Carlos M. Gaspar

Thomas Weston
Samantha Weston
Steven Kent

Jessica Kimball
Jennifer Lane
Willa Carson

Charles Cooper
Jacqueline Roscoe

and
Jack Reacher

The Killing Floor

by Lee Child

1997

I THOUGHT: SHOULD I be worried? I was under arrest. In a town where I'd never been before. Apparently for murder. But I knew two things. First, they couldn't prove something had happened if it hadn't happened. And second, I hadn't killed anybody.

Not in their town, and not for a long time, anyway.

"So let's talk about the last twenty-four hours, [Reacher]," he said.

I sighed. Now I was heading for trouble.

"I came up on the Greyhound bus," I said.

"Where did you get on the bus?" he asked me.

"In Tampa," I said. "Left at midnight last night."

"Tampa in Florida?" he asked.

I nodded. He rattled open another drawer. Pulled out a Greyhound schedule. Riffed it open and ran a long brown finger down a page. This was a very thorough guy.

CHAPTER ONE

FBI SPECIAL AGENT CARLOS Gaspar lounged back in the driver's seat of the rental sedan to stretch his bad right leg, but all senses remained fully alert. The last time he'd been on MacDill Air Force Base, Gaspar's partner had been wounded and a man had died resisting routine arrest. It was his sixth sense that rankled. He had a bad feeling about the place. He couldn't shake it.

He'd chosen the center lane and pulled into place behind a line passing steadily through the guard stations. One SUV ahead now, sporting a patriotic car magnet.

Veteran, probably.

Once upon a time, a veteran could be trusted to follow protocol. Veterans knew the rules. Knew they couldn't bring personal weapons on the base or enter restricted areas. They didn't need to be watched. But increasingly, veterans and even active military seemed to be going off the rails now and then.

Sometimes for good cause.

Reacher was a veteran. Gaspar never allowed himself to forget that.

He preferred the smaller Bayshore Gate entrance. Closer to their destination. Less traffic. Only one lane. Only one sentry. Ruled out for just that reason: Because that sentry had fewer vehicles to inspect, she'd be more likely to ask thorough questions Gaspar would not answer. Which would probably land him in the brig and he didn't have time for that today.

The main gate entrance to Tampa's MacDill Air Force Base was less treacherous because he could get lucky. Three traffic lanes fed into the main gate. Each lane supported two security stations configured to more closely resemble drive-through windows at a prosperous suburban bank than a military checkpoint.

Except bank tellers don't wear BDUs and side arms.

Base security handled 20,000 people passing through every day as a matter of routine. Today was not routine. Which meant security would be relaxed, maybe.

From behind aviator sunglasses, Gaspar watched the security process unfold predictably around him. But the whole setup of the event felt wrong. Too much lead time since the target's attendance was announced, for one thing. Too public. Too many people. An unpredictable target with too many enemies and too many secrets.

And the usual dearth of good Intel about everything.

It was a bad combination and he didn't like it, even without factoring Reacher into the equation.

Not that it mattered to the Boss what Gaspar liked or didn't like.

The flashing sign outside the security checkpoint declared Force Protection Condition Alpha, meaning only slightly elevated security in place. Probably bumped up a notch because of expected increased civilian attendance at the annual memorial service honoring deceased members of military families, he figured. He took that as a good omen. The base commander couldn't feel as uneasy as Gaspar did or security would be tighter.

He palmed his plastic VA card and flipped it through his fingers like a Las Vegas card shark, then tapped it rapidly on the steering wheel as if that would encourage the security personnel to speedier service. The Boss said Gaspar's VA card would serve as required military ID to enter the base because of the hundreds of people expected at the memorial ceremony. Gaspar figured the Boss had greased the wheels to make it so, as he usually did.

Gaspar glanced over at his current partner to confirm that she wasn't freaking out any more than usual. "How late are we?"

He'd bought the aviators months ago to block the blinding glare of Miami sunlight. Now, they also served to shield him from her penetrating evaluation of his every move.

His shades weren't needed at the moment, as it happened. "Twenty-five minutes," FBI Special Agent Kim Otto replied, without lifting her gaze from her smart phone's screen.

He'd found Otto's nuanced perception almost telepathic in the weeks since the Boss had paired them up for reasons unknown. They worked well together. He liked her. She seemed to like him well enough. The partnership was improving.

But he was still wary.

Otto's self-preservation instincts never relaxed. Not for half a moment. Ever.

He had a family to support. And twenty years to go. And this was the only field assignment he'd been offered since his disabling injury. Playing second on the team to a woman ten years greener added to the insult. Yet he felt grateful to have the work, mainly because it was the only option he had.

But the Reacher job was more dangerous than they'd been told. Much more. As a result, Otto was jumpier than a mosquito on steroids. She would replace him in a hot second if she became the slightest bit concerned about his reliability.

And she'd be smart to cut him out. He'd do the same to her if their roles were reversed. Maybe even as their roles were now.

So he had to be careful. Safer that way.

Which meant he needed as much distance as he could summon inside the sedan before she sensed any danger.

Why was it so hot in here? He flipped up the fan speed on the air conditioning.

The security staffer took three steps back from the SUV in front of them and the vehicle passed through. Gaspar raised his foot off the brake and allowed the sedan to roll forward until his window was even with the security officer.

Gaspar's window remained closed, following the Boss's explicit instructions.

He held up his photo VA card between his left index and middle fingers, almost like a salute. The card had a bar code on it. If the security guard followed procedure, she'd scan the card. He waited. She did, and waved him through without hassle. The scan was routine. The data should get lost in the mountain of data collected every day. As long as Gaspar did nothing to draw attention to himself, his presence here today should remain undiscovered by the wrong people. He hoped.

He let the sedan roll on through the checkpoint, releasing a breath he hadn't known he'd been holding. If they'd been required to offer FBI badges or answer questions, or if security had searched the sedan, everything would have become a lot more complicated. His life was already complicated enough.

As much as they relied upon the Boss's promise of lax

security in their case, he felt Otto's disapproval emitting like sonar waves. How many other VA cards had been waved through today? Was Reacher's one of them? And who checked the civilians required only to show their drivers' licenses for this special event?

But they'd passed the first hurdle. They were on base. Unidentified. So far, so good.

CHAPTER TWO

THE BOSS HAD SAID their movements would be unrestricted inside the gate. Except for certain areas where armed guards were posted. It would be easy enough to avoid those.

"Notice anything worrisome since you were here last?" Otto asked.

He glanced her way. She had her head turned to look out her window, scanning for threats, probably. Especially from behind, she looked like a tiny Asian doll. The top of her deceptively fragile-looking shoulder rested well below the bottom edge of the big sedan's window. If she hadn't put that alligator clamp on her seatbelt at the retractor, it could have sliced her head off her neck in an accident.

"Well?" she said, more insistent this time, scanning through the front windshield now. When he still didn't reply, she glanced his way.

He shrugged, combed his hair with splayed fingers, turned his head and made a show of looking around.

MacDill Air Force Base was both a country club for military families and a war zone. A strange combination of all-inclusive resort and weaponized death star. It boasted a beach and golf course and a full-featured campground for veterans dubbed "Famcamp," where his last trip here had ended in disaster. Inside the buildings you'd find standard Government Issue everything. Then there were the heavily armed guards protecting the strategic commands that earned the base its lofty importance to national defense and control over state-of-the-art killing machines around the world.

Before his injury, Gaspar brought his kids to the annual MacDill AirFest. He'd been here on special assignments while he was in the army, and once or twice since he'd been assigned to the FBI's Miami Field Office. He hoped today's arrest would go more smoothly than his last one here.

"It's a simple question, Chico," Otto said, continuing her recon.

"Wish I had a simple answer." He took in the view through the glass again—right, left, front and in the rear view mirror—seeking any unfamiliar additions to the geography.

The base consumed every inch of the small peninsula jutting out into Tampa Bay. The last time he'd been here it was to attend a retirement dinner in the officers' club, which had since been demolished. Nothing abnormal in that. When new facilities were required, it generally meant old stuff was demolished and replaced.

Today's event was a perfect example. Hundreds of civilians were expected at a temporary outdoor stage like it had always been there. The chosen site was close to the Strategic Operations Command Memorial Wall honoring the fallen. Nearby, multiple command centers for war. Death and life combined in paradise, to jarring effect.

"What time is Weston scheduled to be arrested?" he asked.

"After the service," she said, checking her Seiko. "Maybe three hours from now. Plenty of time to get what we came for and get out before the arresting agents move."

"Plenty of time for all sorts of things to happen." He shrugged as if unconcerned, but figured she knew better.

Building a current file on Jack Reacher—filling in the blanks after he'd left the Army's 110th Special Investigations Unit—had seemed routine initially. Until they read the background file, which was thin. Too thin. Since, they'd been pulling the scabs off old wounds Reacher had caused. It meant infiltrating enemy territory every time. Both Gaspar and Otto had fresh scars to prove it.

No reason to believe Weston would be an easier interview subject than the others had been. In fact, from what they'd learned about the man, there was every reason to believe he'd be worse.

They'd been warned to watch out for Reacher, who came, destroyed and departed like a liger. Neither he nor Otto needed to be reminded to watch for him, but Gaspar wanted to believe it unlikely Reacher would try to get Weston today. Their feud was sixteen years old and surely even Reacher might have lost track of Weston in all that time.

"Weston has stayed out of Reacher's way all this time," Otto said. "So why is Weston sticking his neck out by attending this particular memorial ceremony? He could have come any time. The base holds these generic memorials for military family members to pay their respects every year. Weston contacted them a month ago and said he wanted to attend this particular service. It doesn't make any sense, does it?"

"Not to me," Gaspar replied. "So we do what we do."

"Meaning what?"

"Meaning we stay alert. We're missing something important, Sunshine."

Her tone was hard in reply. "So what else is new?"

Gaspar parked the sedan an assured clear distance from civilian traffic around the memorial site, which seemed to have a disproportionate number of handicapped parking spaces, and they stepped out into the warm November sunshine.

Gaspar stretched like a lizard. After the past few weeks in frigid cold, he'd forgotten how good Florida sunshine could feel a few days before Thanksgiving.

Otto watched him from just over the hood of the sedan, but said nothing.

When he stepped around the car, they began walking toward the memorial site, keeping a few yards' distance from other early arrivals. Some were in wheelchairs. Some moved jerkily on new prosthetic limbs. One mystery solved: the excess of handicapped spaces. The memorial service was an annual event to honor fallen members of military families. Many attendees were wounded veterans themselves.

Gaspar's limp was pronounced at first, but eased with exercise, as it usually did.

"I know you're running through it again in your head," Gaspar said with a grin to distract her from his limping. "Just verbalize for me while you're at it. Another run-through never hurts."

She scowled as if he'd falsely accused her. He hadn't. She never stopped thinking, analyzing, crunching data in her head, even if it was the same data, over and over. He didn't complain. Her odd habits had already saved his ass more than once.

"The subject is retired Army Lieut. Col. Alfred Weston." She rattled off the few important facts they'd received in the

Boss's materials: "Sixteen-plus years ago, Weston was posted here on a classified assignment. No details in the file. Weston's wife and three children were murdered. Reacher somehow became the lead Army investigator on the case. He thought Weston was the killer."

"Why?"

"Who knows?" she said, as if she was slightly irritated at Reacher's unfathomable behavior. Which she probably was.

"But Reacher couldn't prove Weston did it," Gaspar continued for her, "and it turned out the real shooter was arrested quickly by the locals." He fingered the Tylenol in his pocket. He'd swallow another one when she wasn't watching. His doctors prescribed narcotic pain medication, but he couldn't risk taking it. Tylenol was the strongest thing he'd allow himself while they were working.

She said, "After the killer's arrest, the official investigation of Weston ended."

"Unofficially, Reacher wouldn't let it go," Gaspar went on. Reacher never let anything go once he had his teeth into it. Otto was the same way. For sheer bulldog tenacity, Reacher and Otto were as alike as bookends.

"Weston's been living abroad," Otto said, "Middle East mostly, since he left the Army under a cloud of Reacher's making." She stopped talking abruptly, as if she didn't want to mention the rest.

Gaspar's right leg was feeling stronger. The cramping easing. Limp nearly under control. Pain ever-present, sure, but he could handle pain. He'd been handling it a good long while.

"And now," Otto said, "Weston's accused of major crimes against the U.S. Government. Various forms of corruption, mostly, related to the private security company he operates. A few allegations of using unauthorized force and excessive force. Suspected manslaughter of civilians is at the center of it. A lot of conflicting evidence. Nothing actually proved so far, but plenty to support an arrest and interrogation." She hesitated half a breath. "This is the first time Weston's been on American soil in the past sixteen years."

Same facts he'd memorized on the plane. He hadn't missed anything. He still didn't like it.

Gaspar mulled for a couple more steps before he asked, "Why come back at all? He's got nothing here. Why not just stay offshore and make Uncle Sam send covert operations after him if we wanted him badly enough?"

She shrugged as if the answer didn't matter, when Gaspar knew it did.

"Once they snatch him," she said, "he'll be locked up and off limits to us. We need to get to him today." She took another breath and glanced again at the plain Seiko on her narrow wrist. "We've got less than an hour before the service starts."

Gaspar felt his eyebrows knitting together. Their mission still wouldn't make sense. "Why should Weston tell us anything useful?"

"The Boss says Weston blames Reacher for his troubles and wants to even the score. We're supposed to give Weston that chance and strongly encourage him to take it." Unconsciously, perhaps, she patted her gun under her blazer.

"We're striking out with Reacher's friends so we'll squeeze his enemies instead?" A harsh, dry chuckle escaped Gaspar's lips. "Sounds a little like sticking your head in the mouth of a hungry carnivore doesn't it?"

Otto said nothing.

CHAPTER THREE

THEY'D BEEN ALLOTTED ONE hour to get in, get what they could, and get out without crossing paths with the arresting agents or stepping in another pile of stink from unknown origins. Flight and traffic delays had sucked up more than half of their time already.

"Your gun's loaded, right?" she said, patting hers again as if she didn't realize she'd touched it.

"Come on, Sunshine." He ran both hands through his hair again and stuffed them in his trouser pockets. "We've been over this. We can't discharge weapons we're illegally carrying. Do you have any idea what would happen if we did that?"

"I'm familiar with procedures," she snapped.

"And you're familiar with prison sentences, too."

She seemed unimpressed with his reasoning. "Weston's made enemies here and around the world. A few have a strong appetite for vengeance."

Gaspar knew she was worrying about one particular enemy. So was he.

"Unlikely Reacher knows Weston's here," he said. "How

would he have heard? The man's far enough off the grid even the
Boss can't find him. Not likely anyone else can."

Finding Reacher wasn't the issue, though. The question was
whether Reacher would find Weston. Or them—a growing
possibility, the longer they went looking for him. Reacher had
friends. By now, smart money said at least one of those friends
had somehow passed along that they were on his trail.

"Reacher lives to piss on the other guy's grave," Otto said.
"He's a highly qualified sniper. The only non-Marine to win the
1000-yard invitational rifle competition."

"It would be crazy to try to kill Weston here where he'll be
so heavily guarded. A good sniper would choose a highway
location. Shoot from a vehicle. Make a clean getaway," Gaspar
said.

Again her hand passed over the lump in her blazer. "I'm
saying we need a Plan B. Guns work for me. Unless you've got a
better plan."

He didn't.

They'd arrived at the ceremony site. Setup was completed
and the audience was slowly filing in. Gaspar estimated seating
for about 1,000 people. A temporary, elevated stage at the front,
a center podium flanked by four chairs on either side. He saw
flat, open parking lots behind the stage where official vehicles
and emergency personnel waited. A dark sedan pulled in from
the opposite side of the parking lot. Which meant there was a
second means of ingress and egress to the area.

One more entrance or escape route to cover. Not ideal.

He studied the site's perimeter. Otto was right. Weston's
tenure here at MacDill, and with the Army in general, had
produced more enemies than most men accumulated in a
lifetime. Yet, today Weston would stand in an open field on an

elevated stage surrounded by too many spots for a moderately good shooter to hide.

It felt foolhardy to Gaspar. Weston had to feel the same way. Any military man would.

Which was one of the things that made the setup feel so profoundly wrong.

Gaspar identified the most likely shelter points for snipers within a seventy yard range. Any military sniper was reliable at five times that distance. There were several good ones and a few more that a sniper as good as Reacher could use to kill and disappear before anyone found his nest. What they had learned about Reacher was that even though he could kill from a distance at any time, he preferred to handle his problems up close and personal. Gaspar had felt like prey every day since he'd received the Reacher assignment. The only reasonable solution was to ignore it and press on.

The base held plenty of weapons and ammo and legitimate personnel who were trained to use them. In theory, all arms were accounted for and all non-security personnel were prohibited from possessing personal weapons on base. In theory.

Like most theories, that one was obviously unreliable. Gaspar knew for sure that at least two people carrying unauthorized weapons were standing in this precise spot already. Seemed to him more than likely there'd be others.

"You know what worries me?" Otto asked.

He laughed. "Everything worries you, Sunshine."

She glared at him. "Why did Weston agree to attend this ceremony, make himself an easy target?"

"I was just wondering that myself," Gaspar said. "Maybe he's got a death wish."

"Or homicidal intent," she said.

Gaspar didn't argue. Either option was possible.

He again checked the potential sniper points he could identify and pointed them out to her. Shooting into a crowd and hitting only the intended target was not a simple thing, but it wasn't impossible, either. The best locations were in the west, with the sun behind him. Firing out of the sun was every sniper's basic preference.

"Just stay out of the line of fire," he told her. "If my partner is shot and killed on a military base, I'll be buried in paperwork for the rest of my natural lifetime. I've got kids to raise."

"Your concern is touching," she said, just before she slugged him in the bicep hard enough to knock him off balance. He righted himself and hammed it up a little to conceal how easily she could fell him.

"Enough horsing around. Be serious for the next ninety minutes, will you?" she scolded.

She was tiny, but fierce. He admired that about her.

Not that he'd let her know it.

Movement near the stage caught his attention. "There's Weston. Let's go."

He set off toward the opposite side of the venue at a good clip. Otto struggled to keep pace at first and then strode past him until it was his turn to struggle. They closed the distance to the edge of the stage where Weston stood at ground level, flanked by a military escort and two women. The escort would be Corporal Noah Daniel, according to the Boss's instructions.

Twenty feet behind Weston stood three bulky civilians wearing navy business suits, white shirts and rep ties, and thick-soled shoes. These could only be private bodyguards. More holes in the "no guns on base" theory, Gaspar figured.

He slowed so Otto reached their target first, allowing Gaspar time to gather quick impressions of the Weston group.

The older woman was Samantha Weston. She was draped in ridiculous fashion garments that probably came from Paris or Milan without benefit of filtering through American good sense.

She was fortyish. Lanky. Lean. Artfully styled hair. Handsomely well-constructed.

Gaspar could spot skilled plastic surgery and *haute couture* across a dim and crowded Miami ballroom. No detective work required here, though. Mrs. Weston's familiarity with both was revealed by Tampa's brutally honest sunlight.

The younger woman standing slightly behind Mrs. Weston was well groomed but plain. Wholesome. Smallish. About thirty, or a couple of years either side, Gaspar guessed. Dark hair. Short, scrubbed fingernails. Everything about her appearance was professionally no-nonsense.

And something else.

She seemed familiar.

A certain lilt to her nose, crinkles around her eyes as she squinted into the sun, dimple in her chin.

Who was she?

Wife of an acquaintance? Ring-less fingers ruled out that option.

Maybe she resembled a celebrity or even a crime victim from a prior case.

He waited a moment for the information to bubble up. No luck. He couldn't place her.

Next, from behind the aviators he scanned the subject like a full body x-ray machine. Weston's dark suit covered him from turkey neck to shiny, cap-toed shoes. All visible body parts were pathetic. Gaspar's scan noted pasty skin, eye pouches, jowls, tremors. Weston was fifty-five, maybe? But he looked every moment of twenty years older.

The expat life in Iraq as a military contractor suspected of murdering local civilians carried its own unhealthy burdens, sure. In Weston's case, the added pressure of surviving the murder of his wife and children on U.S. soil couldn't be easy. Guilt might have gnawed his organs, maybe. Whatever the cause, he looked like he was being eaten alive.

Otto presented herself to them. "Corporal Daniel. Colonel Weston. Mrs. Weston." She hesitated briefly before reaching out to the unidentified younger woman.

"Jennifer Lane," the woman said, extending her hand for a firm shake with Otto first, then Gaspar. "I'm Mrs. Weston's lawyer."

Instantly, Samantha Weston became more concerning. In Gaspar's experience, only people already in trouble and expecting worse trouble traveled with a lawyer.

"I am FBI Special Agent Kim Otto and this is my partner Special Agent Carlos Gaspar. We'd like to talk to Colonel Weston for a few minutes, if you don't mind."

The expression settling on Weston's face was something close to satisfaction. He didn't smile, exactly. More like a smirk. So Weston had expected them. Or someone like them. Which made Gaspar more uneasy than he already was. Why would Weston anticipate that cops would approach him today? The Boss said Weston's arrest was a sting. Gaspar could dream up a dozen explanations, but none of them were good news.

Corporal Daniel performed as ordered. "Mrs. Weston, Ms. Lane, our base chaplain would like a word with you before we begin," he said, leading Samantha Weston away by a firm forearm grip.

Attorney Jennifer Lane followed her client like a pit bull on a leash.

Gaspar positioned himself facing Weston, better to observe and avoid the sniper positions he'd previously noted. Otto stood to one side, also out of identifiable firing lines. Weston remained an easy target and had to know it, but didn't seem to care.

"Sir, we'll only take a few moments of your time," Otto said. "We're hoping you can help us with some background data about the investigating military police officer on your wife's murder case."

"Reacher," Weston said, as though naming an enemy more heinous than Bin Laden. Then, eagerly, "Is he with you?"

Otto's expression, betraying equal parts horror and astonishment at the very thought, was quickly squelched.

Gaspar hid his grin behind a cough. One mystery solved. Weston meant to lure Reacher here today.

And maybe he had. Gaspar didn't find that option comforting in the least.

"We haven't seen him recently," Gaspar said, truthfully enough. He slouched a little and settled his hands into his trouser pockets because it made him seem friendlier. Gaspar knew many successful interrogation techniques, but none of them worked unless the subject wanted to talk. Most of the problem was making them want to. Once they wanted to tell him everything, witnesses were nearly impossible to shut up.

Disappointed that they hadn't served up his quarry, Weston became more suspicious. "Why are you collecting background on Reacher?"

The half-truth rolled more easily off Otto's tongue after weeks of practice, "We're completing a routine investigation."

"Why?"

"He's being considered for a special assignment."

"Cannon fodder? Road kill?" Weston's sharp retorts came fast. "Those are the only jobs Reacher's fit for."

"Meaning what?" Otto asked, unintimidated.

Weston said, "My wife and children were executed. By cowards. While I was serving my country."

"Nothing to do with Reacher, right?" Otto asked.

Weston's face reddened and his eyes narrowed. "Reacher accused me. He arrested me. I wasn't there to see my children buried. I wasn't there to see my wife buried. I sat in a jail cell instead." He clenched and unclenched his fists at his side. "This is the first memorial service I've ever been able to attend for my slain family. You call that nothing? I sure as hell don't."

"Not unreasonable of Reacher, though," Otto said, detached, cool. "Most people are murdered by someone close to them. Anybody who watches television knows that. Reacher wasn't out of line when he considered you a prime suspect."

Weston's chest heaved. He shifted his slight weight and leaned closer to Otto, towering unsteadily over her. She didn't flinch. She remained the polar opposite of cowed. Gaspar figured Weston wasn't used to having any woman stand her ground with him, much less one nearly half his size.

Weston lowered his voice to a mighty pianissimo and still Otto didn't budge even half an inch. "When Reacher found out he was wrong about me? What did he do?"

Otto lifted her shoulders and opened her palms, unimpressed. "I give up."

Otto's behavior enraged Weston a bit more. He leaned in and all but engulfed her like a vulture's shadow. She didn't move and said nothing.

Then, as if he'd flipped some sort of internal switch, he

released the stranglehold on his fists and relaxed his posture. Regular breathing resumed. Sweat beads on his forehead and above his upper lip glistened in the sunlight. A breeze had kicked up, carrying floral scents from the tropical plants in and around the base. A breeze that any good sniper could easily accommodate.

When Weston spoke again, he sounded almost civil, as if Otto had asked him about nothing more personal than last night's dinner menu.

The guy was a sociopath, Gaspar thought. Clearly. Total nut-job. All the signs were there. He'd seen it too many times before.

"It's unfortunate that Reacher's still alive. If I see him before you do, he won't be. Please tell him that for me." His tone reflected the controlled calm Gaspar recognized as subdued rage. A hallmark of stone cold killers, crazy or not.

Gaspar asked, "Why did Reacher think you killed your family? We haven't seen the whole file. Was there some evidence against you?"

"Ask him next time you see him." Weston folded his hands in front of his scrawny abdomen, miming that he had all the patience in the world to do nothing but humor them.

"Right now I'm asking you."

Attendees had been filing in steadily as they talked and now filled the chairs in the audience as well as on the stage. Again, Gaspar noticed a significant number of disabled men and women. Many of them were young. Too young.

Not much time left.

Weston's satisfied smirk turned up a notch. "You work for Cooper, don't you?"

Hearing him utter the Boss's name was a sharp jab, but

Gaspar recognized a classic deflection and refused the bait. Whatever happened after Reacher left the Army, he'd been a good cop. After twenty minutes with Weston, Gaspar was ready to believe anything Reacher reported about Weston on Reacher's word alone.

"Why did Reacher think you'd killed your own family?" Gaspar asked again.

Weston said nothing.

Otto stepped in. "Have you communicated with Reacher since you left the army, Colonel?"

"I've been living abroad."

Otto said, "The globe is a lot smaller than it used to be. People travel."

"Too bad Reacher hasn't been to Iraq." And like that, Weston's control again seemed to snap. "I'd happily kill the bastard. Cooper, too, given the chance."

"What's your beef with the Boss?" Gaspar asked. The guy was crazy, but whatever he thought about the Boss, it was better to find out than get caught napping.

"We all wore the green back then. We were brothers in arms. We were supposed to be taking care of each other. The Army's family, man," Weston said. "You served, didn't you? You've got the bearing. I can smell the green on you. You've gotta know what I mean."

Gaspar did know. He was tempted to make a sarcastic remark about simply surviving being a better outcome than what had happened to Weston's real family. Not to mention the dead and disabled who served under Weston's command. But instead Gaspar said, "Right."

Weston stopped a second to wipe the spittle from the corner of his mouth, to gather himself. When he spoke again, the switch had again been tripped. The controlled calm had returned. "You really don't know, do you?"

"Know what?" Otto asked.

"You can't be that stupid." Weston's lip curled up. The kind of smirk that made Gaspar want to break his face. "Cooper's the biggest snake alive. Always has been. Turn your back and he'll bite you in the ass. Reacher was Cooper's go-to guy. The two of them were behind everything that happened to me."

Gaspar shook his head exaggeratedly, like he'd heard better tales from the Brothers Grimm. "You think Reacher killed your family? On Cooper's orders? Then blamed you?"

"I've had a lot of years to think this through. Cooper and Reacher had a vendetta going against me. It had to be them." He paused, smiling like a demented circus clown. "That's the only possible answer."

Otto intervened. "The hit man said you hired him. He testified you wanted your family killed."

Once again, Weston's agitation resurfaced. The man was like a carnival ride. His face reddened. His eyes narrowed. His lips pressed hard together and he stuck out his chin. "Lies!" he shouted, loud enough for members of the crowd filtering in nearby to hear and turn to stare.

"Close enough for government work," Otto replied without flinching. "You'd been threatened by the gang you tried to rip off. You were told what would happen to your family. You failed to deliver their money. Reacher had nothing to do with any of that."

She didn't mention the Boss had reached out by sending them here today and probably by sending Reacher back then, too. Gaspar wasn't the only one who noticed.

Weston rocked closer and loomed over Otto again. "Little

girl, if you were half as smart as you think you are, you'd have stopped believing Cooper's fairy tales long ago." He lifted balled fists and unclenched his hands, reaching toward her. He looked like he wanted to shake her by her slender neck until she stopped breathing.

Gaspar hoped he'd try. Otto would knock Weston on his ass the second he touched her. But all this talk about Reacher had heightened his tension, too. On the way through security, Gaspar had been concerned. Now, he felt wired tight, ready to snap.

Before Weston had a chance to complete his move, Samantha Weston appeared by her husband's side like a defending Valkyrie from nowhere.

When Weston didn't back down, his wife placed a firm hand on his shoulder. "Tom, darling. It's time."

Otto had yet to move so much as an eyelash. She said in her normal voice, "We'll finish our questions after the service, Colonel."

Weston didn't flinch for another full second. Then he shook off his wife's hand, turned, marched toward the stage, climbed the steps and stood, waiting for Samantha to catch up.

Gaspar and Otto watched in silence until both Westons reached their positions on the stage with the other honorees of the day's service, and then continued to watch them.

The breeze had whipped up to gusty bursts. Unpredictable. Which would make a sniper's job harder. Not impossible. Some would consider the wind a worthy challenge. Reacher was probably one of them.

Eyes still forward, Gaspar said, "I'm okay with staying a while. We've got a few hours before our flight. But what do you think he'll say later that he wouldn't say now?"

"Weston's the first person we've met who is willing to tell

us anything at all about Reacher. I'm not leaving until I hear every last word I can wring out of him." After a full second or so, she asked, "You think the Boss sent us here to see if Weston could actually pin anything on him and Reacher?"

"I gave up trying to guess the Boss's motives years ago." Gaspar nodded in the direction of the entrance, where two males dressed in FBI-normal stood to one side. "More importantly, what are you planning to tell those guys when they ask who we are and what the hell we're doing here?"

"You'll think of something," she replied, focused now on the tableau playing out on the stage. "Who is that reporter talking to Weston?"

CHAPTER FOUR

THE REPORTER WORE A press pass on a chain around her
neck, a video camera slung over her back and a recorder of some
sort raised to capture a conversation Gaspar couldn't hear.
Weston and his wife spoke with her briefly before the lawyer
stepped in and stopped the inquiry. A short verbal exchange
between the reporter and Lane, the lawyer, ended when Lane
herded the Westons to their seats.

Gaspar wondered again where he had seen that lawyer
before. He couldn't place her, but he knew her. He was sure of it.

The reporter raised her camera and snapped a few photos of
the entire scene before she walked down the four steps from the
stage and onto the path directly toward Otto and Gaspar. When
she was close enough, he read her press pass.

Jess Kimball, *Taboo Magazine*.

Odd that *Taboo* would be covering Weston. *Taboo* was in
the vein of *Vanity Fair*, its only real competitor. Gaspar had seen
both magazines around the house because his wife subscribed.
Both covered popular culture, fashion, and current affairs. *Taboo*
was newer, a bit edgier, maybe, but covered the same beat.

Retired military officers were neither of the national glossies'
usual subject or audience. Which made Gaspar more curious
instead of less.

Gaspar stepped in front of the reporter before she walked
past. "Ms. Kimball, a moment of your time?"

Her eyes, when she focused on his, were piercingly blue.
Nostrils flared. "Yes?"

"Why is *Taboo Magazine* interested in Colonel Weston?"

"And you are?" Kimball held the last word in a long, hostile
invitation to reply.

"Carlos Gaspar. FBI. This is my partner, Kim Otto."

Kimball considered something for a moment before she
answered. "Sorry to say, I'm no threat to Weston."

"What's your interest?" Gaspar asked again.

"My mission is to make sure victims get justice. Especially
children."

"What does that mean?" Otto asked.

"Ever heard of Dominick Dunne?"

"The *Vanity Fair* reporter who covered all those infamous
trials after his daughter was murdered," Otto replied.

"I covered Weston's case a while ago when the gunman who
killed Weston's family was executed by the State of Florida.
Weston was living in Iraq at the time. No chance to wrap up with
him until now without traveling to a war zone."

Otto asked, "Why did you say 'the gunman'?"

"He pulled the trigger. But he wasn't the reason those kids
and their mom were murdered. We've got Colonel Weston to
thank for that," Kimball said, in the same way she'd have
thanked Typhoid Mary for robust health.

"Weston denies involvement," Otto said, "and no connection
was established."

The ceremony was opened by a chaplain, who began with an invocation. Those in the audience with the physical ability stood and bowed their heads. Many closed their eyes. Immediate, eerie quiet reigned.

Kimball whispered. "The Army's cop got it right at the outset."

"Reacher?"

A woman nearby raised her head and glared toward them. Otto held her remaining questions until the brief invocation concluded and the audience returned as one to their seats.

Normal squirming set a low, baseline volume beneath which Kimball replied. "Weston's family was murdered because of Weston. He's got their blood on his hands. Doesn't matter who pulled the trigger and killed them in their beds."

"You're the reason the Westons brought a lawyer here today, huh?" Gaspar asked.

Kimball shook her head with a sour smile. "More likely the divorce Samantha's lawyer filed yesterday the second they set foot on U.S. soil," she said. "Either way, the Westons have more than me to be worried about."

"Why do you say that?" Otto asked.

"You wouldn't be here without an agenda." Kimball tilted her head toward the entrance where the two agents waited. "More of your tribe over there. I'm guessing it's not an FBI picnic. Weston's about to get his. Finally. You can be sure I'm here to get photos."

Silence settled over the crowd again, except for a few members who were quietly crying. Occasionally, a brain-injured veteran would speak inappropriately. There were too many brain-injured veterans after the long war. They'd become a part of normal civilian life for military families. Another burden for the stalwart to bear with dignity. Everyone ignored the interruptions.

Still at the side of the stage, Otto, Gaspar, and Kimball were the only people standing. Drawing too much of the wrong attention.

Kimball handed Gaspar her card.

"Call me later. I'll fill you in," she whispered and slipped away to join the other reporters seated near the opposite side of the stage. She was well within her equipment's visual and audio range and beyond the reach of FBI interrogation while the memorial service continued.

CHAPTER FIVE

THE AUDIENCE HAD EXPANDED while Gaspar had been preoccupied by Weston and then Kimball. Seating was now filled to capacity and additional attendees stood blocking the aisles and the exits. His sightline to the official vehicles behind the stage was obscured, but he could see enough to confirm they remained in place. He couldn't see whether Weston's limo and bodyguards were still present, but they probably were.

On the stage, all the chairs were occupied now. Both Westons and the chaplain were seated to the right of the podium. The base commander wasn't present, but the resident Army Military Intelligence unit was represented by a one-star Brigadier General Gaspar didn't know seated to the left of the podium with two civilians. Enlarged photos of the individuals—and, in Weston's case, the family—being remembered today rested on easels blocking Gaspar's sightline to the area behind the seated dignitaries. No one else on Gaspar's side of the stage could see back there now, even if they'd been looking.

Which they probably weren't, because the enlarged photographs magnetized attention like flames drew bugs. The portrait that interested Gaspar declared a near-perfect American family. Five Westons gathered around Dad and Christmas tree, dressed in matching holiday plaids. Meredith Weston perched on the chair's arm, her husband's arm around her waist. She looked maybe thirty-five, blonde and tan with typically perfect American teeth suggesting she'd been a well-loved child once. Three children. All resembled their mother. You could tell the teenaged daughter, covered with freckles and hiding braces, would grow into her mother's beauty. Twin boys sporting fresh haircuts and suits that matched dad's were already little men. Fortunately, the boys looked like mom, too. Even back then, Colonel Weston wasn't handsome.

The photos reminded Gaspar of his own family. Four daughters, and his wife very pregnant with his first son. Gaspar loved his family like crazy. He refused to try to imagine life without them.

Weston's family had ended up dead. How could any father possibly do that? Gaspar had never understood it, even as he knew fathers killed their families every day.

An intent-looking uniformed man was moving toward them along the edge of the audience, his gaze scanning the crowd, but returning to Gaspar and Otto. This would be their contact, an Air Force Office of Special Investigations officer assigned to assist the FBI agents in Weston's arrest after the memorial service ended. Otto spotted him, too, and the three of them stepped away at a safe enough distance from the crowd to talk while maintaining a clear view of the parade ground, as well as the stage and surrounding elements.

"Agents Otto and Gaspar?"

They nodded.

"Did you get what you came for from Weston? We might manage another few minutes before the arrest if you need it."

"Actually—" Otto replied, looking for his name plate.

"Call me Danimal. Everybody does."

"Danimal," she said.

"That's right."

Otto shrugged. "OK, Danimal. I'd like more than just another few minutes with the guy. Two days in a room alone with him, maybe. He knows a lot more than he's telling."

"Sorry. Can't happen," he said. "Happy to spill whatever I know, though. Not that there's much to spill. Reacher was a good cop and he did a good job on the case. He had a good close record on his cases, but he couldn't make it stick against Weston. Everything's in the file. I've read it. We can't release the file, but my boss promised yours that I could answer your questions."

"Not a lot of Army here on base back then, right?" Otto asked. "How was this case Reacher's jurisdiction, anyway?"

"Strictly speaking, it probably wasn't. Weston was on base for a few months on a special assignment. Reacher came down after the murders."

Gaspar asked, "So Reacher wasn't assigned to duty here?"

"No need for Army military police like Reacher. Base security handles everything. In appropriate cases, we coordinate with Tampa P.D. and the local FBI. Sometimes other jurisdictions."

"Weston was Army. What was his assignment?"

"Classified," Danimal said, as if no further comment was necessary.

"Weston lived off base. Why was base security involved in the case?"

"All MacDill security teams have good relationships with local law enforcement. We work together when our personnel are involved."

Otto said, "Reacher disregarded all the standard procedures, I gather."

He nodded. "Murder of an Army officer's family is not the sort of thing we'd keep our noses out of just because it happened off base."

"Weston and Reacher had a history," Gaspar said. "That have anything to do with Reacher's interest?"

Danimal shrugged. "Weston had a history with everybody who crossed his path. He's not an easy guy. You must have noticed."

Gaspar said, "Wife and three kids shot in the head with a .38 while they slept in their own civilian beds around midnight on a Wednesday. Ballistics on the gunshots?"

"It was the wife's gun. First responders found it on the bed still loosely gripped in her hand. Army wives learn to shoot for self-protection and she was damn good at it. In this case, looks like she didn't get the chance to fire."

"Reacher concluded there'd been no intruder?"

"House was in a good, safe South Tampa neighborhood, but shit happens sometimes."

"Not in this case?" Otto asked.

"Right." He nodded. "No forced entry, no identifiable evidence of a break-in. Front door locked and alarm system activated. Family dog asleep in the kitchen."

"The dog slept through the whole thing?" Gaspar asked.

Danimal nodded. "That's what it looked like."

Gaspar had to agree. Dogs don't sleep through break-ins.

Not unless they're drugged, or deaf. Or they know the killer. And sometimes, not even then.

"Say Reacher was right. No intruder," Otto said. "Normal conclusion would be murder suicide. Yet the locals ruled that out and Reacher agreed. Why?"

"No motive, for starters."

Gaspar nodded. Women usually need a reason to kill, even if it's a crazy reason.

"By all accounts, she was a wonderful mother, decent wife to a difficult guy. Kids were great, too. Good students. Lots of friends. No substance abuse."

"All-American family, huh?" Otto asked, glancing again at the photographs on the stage.

Danimal shrugged. "Zero reported difficulties."

Which was not the same thing as no problems, exactly. Gaspar was forming a clearer picture of Reacher's analysis of the crimes. "Suspects?"

"No."

"She have any enemies?"

"None anyone could find."

"How hard did Reacher look?"

Danimal shrugged again. "Not too hard, probably. He knew Weston. We all did. Guy had plenty of enemies. We didn't need to spin our wheels looking for hers."

"Where was Weston at the time of the murders?" Otto asked.

"Alibi was weak from the start," Danimal said. "He claimed he was drinking with buddies at a local strip joint until the place closed."

"Devoted family man that he was. Alibi didn't hold up, though?"

"No confirming surveillance available in those clubs, for obvious reasons. Nobody remembered Weston being there after his buddies left about two a.m."

Gaspar said, "Meaning Reacher focused on the most obvious suspect."

"Pretty much," Danimal said. "Reacher wanted Weston to be guilty, sure. But the rest of us agreed. Reacher wasn't completely wrong."

"Roger that," Gaspar said.

"What happened next?" Otto asked.

Danimal looked uncomfortable for the first time. "That's a little...vague."

"Let me guess," Otto said, sardonically. "Weston was hauled in looking like he'd been run over by a bus, right?"

Danimal shrugged and said nothing.

"What persuaded Reacher to abandon charges against Weston?" Gaspar asked.

Silence again.

Otto asked, "So what happened after Weston's arrest?"

"Case was over, as far as we were concerned. The situation moved up the chain of command, out of Reacher's purview. He returned to his regular post."

"Where was that?"

"Texas, maybe?" Danimal said.

"But that wasn't the end of things, was it?"

"Pretty quickly, local detectives concluded Weston's family had been killed by a cheap hit man."

"How cheap?" Gaspar asked.

"Five-hundred dollars, I think, for all four hits."

"Anybody could have paid that," Otto said. "Even on Army wages."

Danimal didn't argue. "They couldn't tie Weston to the killer, so charges against Weston were dropped. Reacher had no say in the matter. Even if he'd still been on base, the result would have been the same."

Gaspar said, "Reacher had to love that."

Danimal laughed. "Exactly."

Otto tilted her head toward Jess Kimball, who was still sitting with the press off to the opposite side of the stage. "Reporter over there says Weston's family was killed to send him a message. Any truth to that?"

"Probably. But that made him a victim, not a suspect. We couldn't prove anything more," Danimal replied.

"How hard did you try?" Gaspar asked.

"If the evidence was there, Reacher would have found it. He was a good cop and he did a good job on the case."

After thinking a bit, Otto said, "After Weston was released, Reacher kept looking for evidence, didn't he? And he let it be known. He hounded Weston, figuring he'd crack. Or do something else Reacher could charge him for, right?"

Danimal said nothing.

Otto said, "A few of your guys maybe helped Reacher out with that project."

Danimal still said nothing.

Weston was a scumbag through and through. Reacher wouldn't have let that go. Gaspar wouldn't have, either.

"How'd it end?" Otto asked.

"Weston was arrested frequently. Jaywalking. Spitting on the sidewalk. Whatever," Danimal replied.

"Didn't matter as long as Weston was getting hassled and locked up for something and sporting a few bruises, right?" Otto asked.

He shrugged. "When Weston came up for his next promotion, he got passed over. His CO suggested he'd be better off outside, away from, uh, constant surveillance."

"So Weston retired," Otto said.

"Yes."

"And then what?"

Danimal replied, "And then he got worse."

Gaspar figured Reacher had been counting on that. Reacher had sized Weston up and concluded he was a scumbag. Guys like Weston don't get better with age.

While Danimal was briefing them, Gaspar had been preoccupied with Reacher and not watching Weston closely enough. For Gaspar's assignment, Weston was a source of information and nothing more. After he told them what they needed to know, Weston could stand in front of a firing squad and Gaspar wouldn't have cared. Because he agreed with Reacher. Weston killed his family, one way or another. Weston was not the victim here.

Until he was.

CHAPTER SIX

THE SERVICE CONCLUDED. THE chaplain returned to the microphone and asked everyone to stand and bow their heads. Weston, his wife, and the others on the stage did so, along with the audience. Hushed whispers from the respectful crowd stopped. The only noises Gaspar heard were muffled by distance. The chaplain began his benediction.

A split second later, the first gunshot shattered the quiet. Automatically, Gaspar's gaze jerked toward the sniper nests he'd located—was that a rifle's glint he saw snugged up against that HVAC unit?—then back to the stage. He counted two more rapid shots. Like a crazy break dance, Weston's body lurched forward, propelled by the force of each impact from behind, not from any identified nest. Had Gaspar imagined the rifle's glint?

After the third shot, Weston crumpled like a marionette whose strings were abruptly severed.

When Weston fell, he opened a window for the fourth shot, which hit Samantha Weston.

The fifth bullet struck the chaplain.

Gaspar and Otto were already rushing the stage with their

weapons drawn after the third shot, but their sightline behind the stage was still obscured. They'd left Danimal behind with his own weapon drawn, scanning the crowd for the shooter as he got on his radio.

Like a brief time delay on live television, the audience began screaming and chaos erupted just as Otto reached the stage with Gaspar half a step behind. As Gaspar followed her around the left side of the stage, he counted five additional, rapid shots originating from the parking lot behind. Followed by no further shooting.

When they reached the parking lot, two men were down and two more stood over the bodies.

The chaos became choreographed as moves practiced during countless drills were automatically performed almost simultaneously as Danimal's base security took charge.

Weston was approached, triaged, and rushed into one waiting ambulance. Mrs. Weston was rushed to a second ambulance.

The chaplain's injuries were either fatal or minor, judging from the medics' lack of urgency when they reached him.

More security personnel arrived. Two men were confirmed dead.

Within minutes the entire base was locked down. The voice came on the speaker advising everyone to "shelter in place." Meaning hunker down until the situation was secured.

Otto and Gaspar hung back from the working professionals.

"We should go," Otto said, her attention focused on the crime scene. "Those two authorized FBI agents will be around somewhere, maybe calling backup. We can't be caught here."

Though Gaspar agreed, he told her to wait there a minute and slipped around the edges to reach Danimal, who was questioning Weston's bodyguards. The same bodyguards who'd failed to protect their boss. Danimal stepped aside to give Gaspar a brief account of the shooting according to the first witnesses.

"Looks like a lone shooter. That guy," he pointed to one of the two dead men. "No ID yet. He approached the back of the stage about halfway through the service as if he was authorized to be there. When Weston stood for the benediction, he pulled his pistol and shot Weston in the left shoulder, and both legs. Mrs. Weston was shot in the right femur. The other victim is one of Weston's bodyguards. These two guys say the shooter killed their buddy and then they killed him."

Gaspar reviewed the crime scene briefly, then nodded. "It could have happened that way," he said. "Where did they take Weston?"

"He requested Tampa Southern," Danimal said. "Call me later and I'll fill you in. I've got to get back to work."

"Thanks," Gaspar said, then approached the two bodies for a closer look.

The bodyguard lay face down, lifeless, unmoving in a lake of his own blood. Black hair. Bulky guy. Maybe six feet. Maybe 200 pounds of pumped-up shoulders and biceps. Big, but not big enough to stop bullets fired dead on target at close range.

Less than three feet away, the scrawny shooter was face up on the tarmac, one glassy eye still open and the other covered with a black patch. Like several others attending today's memorial, grotesque scars from a healed wound gouged his forehead. One cheek was sunken because half the upper jawbone had disappeared some time ago. His Army BDUs were well worn and oversized for the wasted body inside them. Boots polished but old and scuffed as if he'd had trouble lifting his feet to walk. His deformed right hand still gripped the FN Five-seven pistol he'd meant to use to get up close and execute his target.

Brain injuries manifested in unpredictable ways. It was possible the shooter had been unable to control his homicidal impulses and simply lashed out at the nearest targets, but the whole scene felt darkly, undeniably intentional to Gaspar. Shooting Weston in the back. Shooter knowing he'd die trying to kill. Hitting Weston three times before the two wild shots injured others nearby. A crowd of military families and personnel watching.

It felt very, very personal.

No question the shooter was a man with vengeance on his mind.

But he wasn't Jack Reacher.

Gaspar wondered if Reacher would experience a pang of regret for having his unfinished business with Weston finished for him by this damaged, deranged soldier.

After he'd absorbed all he could about the situation, Gaspar returned to Otto and said, "Let's go."

They slipped weapons back into place and merged with the audience as security herded them to their cars and eventually exited the base though the nearby Bayshore Gate.

While they waited in the long line of traffic, Gaspar told her about the glinting rifle barrel in the sniper's nest, the bodyguard, and the shooter.

"The shooter's definitely not Reacher?"

"Definitely not. Although it could have been him in the nest. Impossible to know."

Otto nodded, thinking. "So. Disabled veteran? Maybe served under Weston's supervision?"

"Iraq has been Weston's location for long enough. They could have crossed paths there, even if Weston wasn't the guy's

CO," Gaspar said. "The shooter was disabled, for sure. Likely a vet. But if we're betting, I'd say he was focused and lucid when he planned and executed this plan."

"Why?"

"Two reasons. First, logistics. Getting close enough to Weston to shoot him required stealth and cleverness, but also logic and planning. He had to get on base, locate the best shooting position, have a weapon, and a long list of other things. None of that could have been accomplished if he'd suffered from a significant mental deficiency."

Otto nodded, considering. "Maybe. One thing we know: the number of vets who suffered head injuries during both Iraq and Afghanistan is staggering. In earlier wars, they wouldn't have survived wounds like that. We can keep so many more alive now, but the treatments aren't great and definitely don't fix the damage."

Gaspar said nothing.

"Sometimes, they suffer strokes and seizures. Behavior can be erratic, even violent," Otto said, running through her internal list of possibles. "Maybe he had a grievance against Weston. And maybe he was just not rational. What's your second thing?"

"He pulled it off. He reached Weston, armed, on a military base designed to stop him. He shot five times before a private bodyguard took him out, but not before he mortally wounded the bodyguard. And he had physical disabilities beyond the head trauma. All of that says logic, planning, knowledge, focus."

Gaspar took a deep breath. Discussions about the abilities of the injured and disabled were bound to lead somewhere he wasn't willing to go. "My money says the guy specifically planned to kill Weston and he was willing to die trying. But with nothing more to go on, it's impossible to know. And, more to the point, not our case. We've got our own problems. So now what?"

"Assuming Weston survives, those two FBI agents will execute his arrest warrant today, no matter what," Otto said. "Let's see if we can get any more out of him about Reacher before we lose the only good lead we've got."

"Okay. But what about Reacher?"

"What about him?"

"If he was the one in that sniper's nest, he knows Weston wasn't dead at the time he got into the ambulance. And he knows where to find Weston now."

"And he's at least thirty minutes ahead of us," Otto said.

Gaspar increased the sedan's speed to tailgate the car in front of them. Maybe today was the day to face Reacher after all. Get some answers right from the source. Finish this assignment and move on.

CHAPTER SEVEN

TAMPA SOUTHERN HOSPITAL WAS located about six miles from MacDill Air Force Base near the opposite end of Bayshore Boulevard. Gaspar stretched out as he settled into the oversized seat and drove along perhaps one of the most beautiful stretches of pavement in Florida.

Immediately outside the Bayshore Gate they passed residential property on the west side of the winding two-lane. At the first traffic light, Interbay Boulevard, more than half the traffic turned west.

Gaspar continued through the residential section, past the streets that led to the Tampa Yacht Club entrances on the right, past Ballast Point. After the next traffic light at Gandy Boulevard, the two lanes separated into a wide divided linear park that ran along the entire shoreline of Hillsborough Bay toward downtown.

Otto seemed to enjoy the scenery, too. As they passed Plant Key Bridge, she said, "I've never been to Tampa before. What's that little island out there?"

"It's called Plant Key. Privately owned. It was originally

built by a railroad baron named Henry Plant."

"He built an island?"

"Well, the Army Corps of Engineers dredged the bay and piled up the dirt, but Plant did the rest. That Moorish looking building was his home, called Minaret. Maybe built in the 1890's. Plant was constructing the Tampa Bay Hotel, now the University of Tampa. He was competing with Henry Flagler for the rich and famous vacationers of the time."

"Don't try to tell me about competition, Chico," Otto said. "I'm from Detroit, where the weak are killed and eaten. There've never been rivals bloodthirstier than the Fords and the Dodge brothers."

He laughed. "Now, there's a great restaurant out there called George's Place. If we get a chance, we'll have dinner there. The chef is amazing."

Otto glanced toward him and smiled for the first time today. "You mean we'd eat something that doesn't come out of a ptomaine cart? What a sweet-talker you are."

He felt a grin sneak up on his lips and some of the unrelenting tension released. "Stick with me, Susie Wong. You ain't seen nothin' yet. You've never tried a gold brick sundae, I'll bet."

When she laughed like that, she seemed younger and prettier, Gaspar realized. She was so serious most of the time that he'd never noticed that about her. She was young. She could still have a normal life with a family. He wondered if she ever thought about that.

"The homes along here across from the waterfront are amazing, too. I've stayed in hotels smaller than that one," she said, pointing to an 8,000-square-foot Georgian-style mansion. "Reminds me of a similar stretch along Lake St. Claire. In

Grosse Pointe, just outside Detroit. I drive out there on weekends sometimes in the summer. Beautiful."

She sounded homesick. Interesting, Gaspar thought. Until now, she'd never seemed to care that she wasn't on her way back for Thanksgiving.

There was no further landmass in Hillsborough Bay until they reached the bridge to Florida Key where Tampa Southern Hospital was located. Gaspar merged onto the bridge and crossed the water before entering the driveway between the hospital and the parking garage.

"Drop me off at the entrance and park the car, okay?" Otto said. "I'll find out what's going on and meet you inside."

"You got it, Susie Wong," he replied. She left the car and he watched her sign in at the information desk and head toward the elevators before he drove to the garage alone.

CHAPTER EIGHT

FOUR PEOPLE OCCUPIED THE small waiting room when Gaspar arrived upstairs. Two men he'd never seen before. Two women he recognized. The men sat a few chairs apart and directly across from the wall-mounted television tuned to a football game. If they noticed or cared about his arrival, they didn't betray themselves.

He was relieved to see both women look up when he entered, which meant he hadn't become invisible since they'd seen him last.

Jess Kimball, the *Taboo* reporter, sat closer to the entrance, as if to ensure she'd be the first to pounce when worthy prey arrived. There was something about her that suggested barely contained anger. Given her feelings about Weston, maybe she was annoyed that the shooter had failed. She was intense, which made Gaspar want to know her story. She was young to be so driven. Usually that kind of idealism came from tragedy and betrayal, in Gaspar's experience. Which was what he figured had happened to her. But what?

The other woman was Jennifer Lane, Samantha Weston's

lawyer. She sat in the corner across from the entry door where she had a clear view of the entire room and its occupants. Gaspar knew a lot of lawyers, but none that were Velcroed to their clients like this one. What was going on there?

He shrugged. Both women were too young to have known Reacher during the Weston murder investigation, which made them vaguely interesting, but irrelevant to his mission.

He absorbed the rest of the scene in a quick glance. One wall of the waiting room featured large plate glass windows overlooking the water. The opposite wall sported a small opening filled with a sliding frosted glass panel behind which, presumably, someone was working. Otto was probably chatting that someone up now. Which was great, because it meant he didn't have to do it.

Gaspar settled into one of the molded plastic chairs, extended his legs, folded his hands over his flat stomach and closed his eyes. The others might think he was sleeping. If nothing interesting happened within five minutes, he would be.

Three minutes later, Otto came in and sat next to him. "I spoke with the Westons' assigned nurse. His name is Steve Kent. He served at MacDill, so he has the necessary clearances, he said. He was also a Navy medic for a while, and respected Weston's service in Iraq. That's why he requested the duty."

"Since when do you need a security clearance to be a civilian nurse to a retired officer?" Gaspar asked without opening his eyes.

"Probably depends on the officer," Otto said. "Anyway, I told him we had a plane to catch and he said he'd take us in as soon as Weston can answer questions."

"Okay," he replied, closing his eyes again. "Did he say anything else I need to know right now?"

Gaspar heard her sigh and imagined she was rolling her eyes, knowing full well what he was up to. Unlike Gaspar, Otto had never been a soldier. She hadn't developed the habit of resting when she could. She got up and left him to it.

When he checked through his lashes, he saw her pacing the room, stopping now and again to glance out the window at Bayshore Boulevard. On a clear day, Gaspar knew she could have seen Plant Key and George's Place and probably all the way to MacDill at the opposite end of the linear park. Not today. Heavy clouds had moved in, bringing congested air that obscured the sightline. He settled his eyes truly shut.

Gaspar figured even if Reacher was in the vicinity, he couldn't reach Weston as long as Weston was still in surgery. Gaspar might have dropped off for a quick twenty winks, but he heard Otto engage in subdued conversation with one of the women. Probably Kimball. Reporters were chatty by nature. Probably not Lane. Lawyers were notoriously tight-lipped. Trying to talk to Lane would be a waste of time. Whatever Otto found out from whoever she was talking to, she'd tell him eventually. He let his breathing flatten and even out as he felt himself dropping again toward sleep.

He was almost there when the door opened and Gaspar raised his eyelids enough to see a woman dressed in pink surgical scrubs enter. "You're the FBI agents?" she asked.

"That's right," Otto said, directing her to the seat next to Gaspar and leaving Kimball and Lane behind her looking miffed at being excluded.

"I'm Trista Blanke, O.R. Patient Coordinator," she said. "I've been told I should give you an update on Mr. and Mrs. Weston. They should both be out of surgery shortly. Mr.

Weston's most serious wound was the shot to the back of his shoulder. The bullet traveled through his body, which is better than most alternatives. But it nicked an artery. He lost a lot of blood and the repair surgery lasted a bit longer than it otherwise would have."

"And Mrs. Weston?" Otto asked.

"She was wounded in the right thigh. Again, the bullet traveled through, but it shattered the femur. She should be fine once reconstruction is completed," she said. "They'll be in recovery for an hour or so after the procedures."

"When can we talk to them?" Otto asked.

"When they're out of surgery, you can give it a try. But until the anesthesia wears off, they may not make much sense."

"Thanks," Otto said.

"No problem," she said before she approached Jennifer Lane, likely to deliver the same news. Kimball crowded in to hear.

"We are probably wasting our time," Otto said, quietly.

Gaspar didn't argue. Except for the possibility of running into Reacher, he figured their time could be much better spent eating. He settled back into his waiting posture and reclosed his eyes, hoping for a quiet five minutes.

When Ms. Blanke had completed her mission and advanced toward the exit, Gaspar heard Otto join her, asking, "Where can I get a cup of coffee?"

Four minutes, forty-five seconds later, the football game ended and the two guys who'd been watching left the room. Gaspar was now alone with the two women. In his bachelor days, he'd have considered that a fringe benefit of the job.

Jessica Kimball spoke first. "Are you planning to arrest both Westons when they come out of recovery?"

"What reason do you have for arresting Samantha Weston?" Jennifer Lane demanded.

Kimball replied, "He's FBI. The Asian woman, too. Why else would they be here?"

"Is that true?" Lane asked.

Gaspar's eyes remained closed and he said nothing. Otto would have bristled at the assumption she was Asian. Oh, sure, she looked like her Vietnamese mother. But she considered herself 100% tall, blonde, sturdy, stubborn German, like her father. Gaspar grinned and said nothing.

Kimball walked over and kicked the sole of his right shoe. Not hard. Just enough to jostle a normal person to attention. But the strike sent painful shock waves up his right leg and into his right side where the muscles had collapsed and the nerves touched things they weren't meant to touch.

"You're not sleeping," Kimball said.

"Checking my eyelids for holes," he replied, willing his pain to settle down. Which never worked. Biofeedback was bunk. Maybe pain was in the brain, but despite his exercise of will, his leg settled into the dull thumping he'd long ago accepted as normal. He opened his eyes, but didn't alter his posture. "What can I do for you, Ms. Kimball?"

"Same thing the FBI has been doing for me for a decade," Kimball said, bitterly. "Nothing."

Lane cut in belligerently. "Do you have an arrest warrant for Samantha Weston? You intend to arrest her while she's incapacitated and unable to understand her rights, Agent Gaspar?"

"Obviously, she understands she has a right to an attorney, since you're here," Gaspar replied without moving. "The only way your presence here makes any sense to me is that she's been expecting us. Which means someone tipped her off. When I find out who did the tipping, you may have yourself another client."

The expression on Lane's face suggested he'd hit the bullseye. Most leaks were intentional. If someone had warned Samantha Weston of her impending arrest, the notice was tactical. Which made him wonder briefly, as a matter of professional curiosity, what the local agents were really up to with Weston. If they already had a warrant supported by probable cause for arrest, why did they want his wife?

"Maybe I don't need your client, Ms. Lane. I'm only interested in the original murder investigation," Gaspar said. "What do you know about that?"

"Samantha wasn't living in Tampa back then," Jennifer Lane replied. "Nor was I."

Kimball said, "I've investigated thoroughly for *Taboo*, and I was at the gunman's execution. So I probably know more than she does."

The waiting room door opened again and Otto entered with four cups of black coffee. Everyone took a cup and spent a few moments adding and stirring.

Lane sipped and swallowed before she asked, "Are you thinking today's shooting is somehow about that old case?"

"What do you think?" Gaspar replied.

"I doubt it," Otto said. "Seventeen years is a long time for any normal person to carry a grudge."

Like a woman with personal experience, Kimball said, "Not where your kids are concerned, it isn't."

"Say you're right," Lane said to her. "What do you think is going on here?"

Jennifer Lane looked young and inexperienced. How'd she

get a powerhouse client like Weston's wife? Curious situation, at the very least, Gaspar thought again.

Jess Kimball was about the same age as Lane, but she seemed more worldly somehow. As if she'd been through tough times that had aged her and forged her titanium spine. She said, "We need to know how today's shooter is connected to Weston. It wasn't a random shooting, because the guy went right up to Weston and fired only at him. When we get the name of the shooter, I should be able to tell you what's going on."

"What makes you so sure?" Otto asked.

"I do very thorough research, Agent Otto. If Weston's sneezed in the wrong direction, I've found out about it," Kimball said, clearly miffed at the perceived slight to her reporting skills. "Listen: this guy is a miserable human being who's caused nothing but heartache wherever he's gone. This wasn't the first time someone has tried to erase Weston from the planet. He's had more lives than an alley cat already. Sorting through the list of people waiting in line for a chance to kill him will take some time."

Before Otto had a chance to reply, the waiting room door opened again. Every time it happened, Gaspar tensed a bit. Expecting Reacher. But so far, he hadn't materialized.

This time, four people entered ahead of a short, stout man dressed in hospital scrubs. The smallish waiting room was instantly overcrowded.

Gaspar recognized the two FBI agents he'd seen at the memorial service intending to arrest Weston for a laundry list of crimes against the government. Lane and Kimball weren't too far off in their assessment of the FBI's intentions, though they had been led a bit astray regarding the identity of the Bureau's official team for the arrest.

There was an awkward moment while everyone seemed blinded by the unexpected presence of the others before the stout man in scrubs began threading his way through the group on his way to the interior door. One of the agents stopped his progress by pulling out his badge wallet. "I'm Special Agent Edward Crane and this is Special Agent Derek Bartos." Crane, Gaspar thought. He knew—and didn't much like—the man. "We're here to take recorded statements from Thomas Weston and his wife, Samantha Weston." Crane pointed toward one of the other two newcomers, a tall redhead wearing jeans and blazer over a white tee-shirt and a pixie hair cut suitable for a woman ten years younger. "This is Judge Willa Carson and her court reporter, Ms. Natalie Chernow."

Gaspar's right eyebrow shot up. There weren't that many Federal judges in Florida and he'd met most of them several times—the FBI and the federal bench routinely worked cooperatively. Judge Carson's jurisdiction was the Middle District of Florida, though, and Gaspar generally stayed in his own sandbox in the Southern District, so he'd never met her.

But he'd heard stories about the freewheeling Willa Carson, who was said to care less for precedent and statutes than her own version of appropriate justice. Some said Carson's conduct was unjudicial. Others said she was a breath of fresh air. All of which, for a law-and-order man like Gaspar, wasn't usually good news. But he'd mellowed lately on the rule-following. He could hardly fault Judge Carson for doing the same.

The stout man spoke up. "I'm Steven Kent, physician's assistant assigned to both patients. Colonel Weston is out of surgery and stable, though he's too groggy to answer questions yet. He'll be moved in about thirty minutes." His tone was not exactly disrespectful, but he wasn't deferential, either. "Mrs.

Weston should be moved by then as well. I'll let you know."

Kent turned smartly like a soldier on parade and left without further comment. Brief silence reigned.

Otto stood and introduced herself and Gaspar to the new arrivals before she said, "There's a coffee pot at the station across the hall. Anybody interested?"

Jennifer Lane held out her empty cup and said, "I'd love another one. Would you mind? I'd come with you, but I need to watch these new guys."

Bad move. She'd insulted the FBI, which raised Otto's hackles along with those of the other agents. Gaspar remained unruffled. Lawyers were always sanctimonious, in his experience. Being a lawyer herself, Otto couldn't very well say so. Gaspar hid his grin as she grudgingly collected Lane's cup.

"I'm fine," Kimball replied.

"Judge Carson? Coffee?" Otto offered.

Carson moved to join her, towering over Otto and glancing back as they headed for the door. "Surely you people can play nice until I get back. If not," she looked Gaspar in the eye, "go ahead and shoot them all."

Gaspar laughed out loud. Yep. Judge Willa Carson might be worth the drive up from Miami on the right case. He'd keep the idea in mind. If he ever got back to his normal job.

CHAPTER NINE

AFTER THE DOOR CLOSED behind Otto and the Judge, Crane said, "Agent Gaspar, can I have a word with you outside, please?"

Gaspar stood, stretched, ignored the pain and forced himself not to limp as he followed Crane into the corridor. When they reached the window at the end of the hallway where they were unlikely to be overheard, Crane asked, "What are you doing here, Gaspar?"

"Enjoying the sunshine."

"Still the same smart ass."

"I think you mentioned that the last time our paths crossed, Crane."

"When I saw you at the memorial, I called in. Miami doesn't know why you're here. Have you gone rogue, Gaspar?"

"Possibly," he replied.

"If you're connected to Weston, you're going down. Got that?"

Gaspar ignored the threat, which was par for the course with Crane. "Rumor says you've got a warrant in your pocket.

Brought along the judge herself, just to cover your bases. The bad news, though: you arrest Weston, you won't need a court reporter. He's not talking to you until he gets a lawyer, and probably not then."

"He's got a lawyer, and he'll talk."

"Lane says she's the wife's lawyer. Not his," Gaspar said.

"Not to me, she didn't." If he jutted his chin any farther, he might fall over from the weight of his fat head.

"You're thinking Weston's going to confess to something? Have you ever talked to the guy? He wouldn't tell you how he takes his coffee unless he had a damn good reason."

"He must have a good reason, then."

Gaspar hadn't considered that Weston would confess. He mulled this over, pushed the idea this way and that, like kneading bread. Couldn't make it work.

"What reason?"

"Don't know. Don't care." Crane sounded like a guy grunting his way through the defensive line. "He's committed about a hundred counts of treason. Murder. Grand larceny. You name it. The guy's a scum-bucket. I get it on the record in front of a Federal judge before he croaks, that's all I care about."

"You think Weston is dying? You're planning a dying declaration?" Gaspar laughed a good two seconds before he controlled himself. "He was winged. Two busted legs and a messed up shoulder. That's it. He's not dying. You're wasting your time."

"Wise up. He's got cancer. He'll be dead by the end of the month. It's his wife he's worried about protecting now. He thinks we'll charge her with his crimes."

"Why would he think that?"

Crane shrugged and made no reply. Which was all the reply

Gaspar needed. Crane must have threatened to charge Weston's wife. And Weston must have believed the threat. Nothing else would puff Crane's confidence up so far.

Steven Kent came around the corner and saw them standing at the end of the hallway. "You can come in now," he said, then stuck his head into the waiting room and made the same announcement to the others.

"What about Weston's wife?" Gaspar pressed.

"That's his motivation. He's trying to save her ass," Crane said.

Gaspar wondered whether the wife cared that much about Weston, since she'd filed for divorce. He shrugged. "Will it work?"

"Depends on what he says, doesn't it?" Crane strode away from Gaspar like a man who'd spiked the ball in the end zone.

CHAPTER TEN

THEY CROWDED AROUND WESTON'S hospital bed in a
large, open recovery room that had been cleared of all patients
except Weston and his wife. She was obviously still out cold, but
Weston was at least approaching consciousness—quietly
moaning, eyelids fluttering. A blanket covered him from the
waist down, obscuring the state of reconstruction done to both
legs. His shoulder was bandaged, but not casted. Gaspar guessed
the repairs were done on the inside.

Unless he perked up pretty markedly, they weren't going to
get much of a statement from him. And even if they did and he
said something worthwhile, it wouldn't carry much weight later,
given the amount of drugs in his system. Undeterred, Natalie
Chernow, the court reporter, had set up her machine near the
head of the bed to be sure she accurately heard and recorded
anything he might babble. She also activated a tape recorder.
Belt and suspenders, Gaspar supposed.

Judge Carson stood at the foot of the bed, the better to see
and hear everything as it happened, should anything happen.

Lane said she would act as Weston's representative for the

purpose of the statement so they didn't have to call in another lawyer, which wasn't exactly kosher. But nothing about the situation was normal and it wasn't Gaspar's case, so he wasn't going to object. Even though he'd like to whip that "I told you so" smirk off Crane's face.

Lane stood next to the court reporter, Crane and his crony Bartos stood across the bed from Gaspar and Otto, and Kimball pressed herself into position beside them.

"Wait," Lane said to her. "What the hell are you doing in here?"

"First Amendment and Florida's Sunshine law. Press would be allowed in a courtroom for the statement," Kimball pointed out, "so I can't be excluded just because proceedings are in a hospital."

Lane appealed to Judge Carson, who ruled that Kimball could stay. Gaspar and Otto, too. Carson offered no explanation for her ruling.

Gaspar didn't expect to learn much, especially since Weston had so far only managed the occasional groan, though it made sense to play things out just in case he got chatty. You never knew. It was just barely possible he might cough up a lead on Reacher that he and Otto could follow up later. Mainly they stayed because it would have looked odd to leave at that point.

And then Weston opened his eyes. When he saw Gaspar, his mouth opened in a wide, drugged, silly smile. His pupils were dilated and his speech slurred when he gleefully asked, "Did my guys get him?"

"What?" Otto asked, leaning in.

Weston's voice was weak, whispery, hard to hear. But unmistakably cheerful. "Reacher. Shot me. Did my guys kill him? Is he dead?"

Otto asked, "You lured Reacher to the memorial so your bodyguards could kill him?"

Crane glared at Otto, but she didn't see him. Crane spoke up. "Colonel Weston, the shooter was Michael Vernon. He was killed at the scene. You knew him, right? He served under you in Iraq for two years. Hit by an IED, remember? Two buddies died. Vernon survived. Blamed you for the whole thing, would be my guess."

Weston sank into his pillows and closed his eyes again. His breathing became more ragged. Steven Kent must have noticed something irregular on the monitors because he came into the room and checked the machines.

"Ten minutes. No more," he said to Crane. "Otherwise, he won't survive the night."

"You said his injuries weren't life threatening," Crane said.

Kent stood his ground, "I said normally not life threatening. We need to keep it that way, don't you think?"

Crane didn't like it, but he backed off. Gaspar figured Crane's restraint wouldn't last long.

But it was true that Weston looked bad. When he found out his plan to kill Reacher failed, his fragile strength seemed to evaporate. Gaspar wondered how many times Weston's vendetta against Reacher had failed before. Weston's reach was extensive, inside the government and out. Another possible explanation for Reacher's hiding so far off the grid that not even a bloodhound could find him. At least until Reacher could take care of Weston or something else got Weston first. Which didn't seem so paranoid right at the moment.

The court reporter announced she was ready.

Judge Carson started the proceedings by opening the record and covering all the legal necessities. She said she'd granted an emergency motion for a recorded statement from Mr. and Mrs. Weston because the FBI represented to her that the statement was essential to an ongoing criminal investigation likely to be harmed if Mr. and Mrs. Weston became incapacitated.

And because Weston's counsel consented.

Jennifer Lane made a short statement about the limited nature of her legal representation and her clients' consent. Observers said nothing.

Finally, Crane began his questions. He could have spent the ten minutes he'd been allotted following up on Weston's plan to kill Reacher, which was the only thing Gaspar was interested in hearing about, but instead his questions focused on Weston's private security company operating in Iraq. Each question was accusatory and belligerent, Gaspar thought. Maybe a little desperate. But it didn't matter. Crane was destined to get nowhere.

Weston had exhausted his available energy on Reacher. Now, he was mostly non-responsive. He grunted a couple of times to signal yes or no. He moaned. He seemed to be almost unconscious. Ms. Chernow's transcript would be mostly a list of questions followed by empty spaces.

After the promised ten minutes, Steven Kent returned to check his patient. "I'm sorry, but that's it. Colonel Weston isn't able to continue."

Crane's annoyance was on full display. "But we're not finished."

Kent replied, "For now you are. You can come back in a couple hours and try again if you want. Or you can call me if you don't want to make an unnecessary trip."

Crane opened his mouth to argue again, but Judge Carson said, "Thank you, Mr. Kent. We'll close the record at this time and resume later this evening or as soon as Colonel Weston is capable."

Crane said, "Let's question Mrs. Weston now, then."

Samantha Weston was in the room's only remaining bed. A curtain separated her bed from her husband's. Kent pulled the curtain back and checked her health indicators. He shook his head. "Mrs. Weston is still sedated. She's not able to communicate at this time, either, I'm afraid."

Crane's mouth was set in a hard line. Gaspar watched him fight to control his anger. He was a pouter, this guy. Too soft. When he didn't get his way, he was whinier than Gaspar's ten-year-old daughter. The thought made Gaspar smile and Crane glared back as if he might start a fistfight. Gaspar struggled not to laugh. He caught Otto's eye and saw her reaction was the same as his.

Judge Carson saw the lay of the land. She did what judges do. She wrapped it up. "Is there anything else anyone wants to put on the record at this time?"

No one raised anything. She closed the record and everyone left the room except Ms. Chernow, who stayed to pack up her equipment.

In the corridor, Crane seized the initiative again. "Judge, we'd like to continue in two hours. We're worried that these witnesses won't survive the night. If they don't, our case will be irreparably harmed—"

Judge Carson headed him off before he could get too amped up. "Fine. Ms. Chernow exists on nuts and dried fruit she carries in her purse. On that diet, I'd be dead in a week, and I'm hungry. Anyone want to join me for dinner at George's Place? No need to change clothes. We can grab a quick bite in the Sunset Bar."

Because refusing a dinner invitation from the judge on your

case wasn't a smart move, everyone officially interested in Weston should have accepted.

But Crane said, "I need to review my file to streamline my questions. I'll just grab something from a vending machine."

Agent Bartos, probably figuring it would be a bad career move to contradict his boss, pulled out his wallet and left for the nearest sandwich.

Jennifer Lane seemed torn by indecision. If she stayed, she could keep an eye on Agents Crane and Bartos, but she'd have to stop watching Gaspar and Otto. Not to mention ticking off the Judge on her case. If she went to dinner, though, Crane and Bartos would remain unsupervised and who knows what mischief they'd get up to without her to restrain them.

Gaspar stifled his smirk and glanced over toward Otto, who pretended to yawn, probably to cover amusement.

"I'm in," Jess Kimball announced.

Otto said, "Me, too." Who knew why? Her motives were usually a mystery to Gaspar.

No mystery at all regarding Gaspar's motivation for accepting Judge Carson's invitation. She'd offered to buy and he was hungry. Simple as that.

CHAPTER ELEVEN

JUDGE CARSON'S MERCEDES CLK convertible zipped along Bayshore Boulevard like a homing pigeon on its return flight. Jessica Kimball's SUV followed. Gaspar brought up the rear in the rented sedan.

George's Place was the only five-star restaurant in South Tampa, as far as Gaspar knew. He'd never eaten at another one. Which might not mean anything. He didn't come to Tampa often and he wasn't a big foodie. A good Cuban sandwich was good enough for him. And any dessert made with guava.

The effortless drive from Tampa Southern to the Plant Key location was as beautiful tonight as it had been earlier in the day. Bayshore Boulevard beribboned the water's edge along the miles in both directions. The full moon and lighted balustrade created a warm, magical picture his daughters always loved.

"How about a quick recap?" Otto asked, as if she were actually giving him an option.

"Sure."

She ticked off her conclusions raising one finger at a time as if they were facts. Which they probably were. "Weston put the

word out and staged his attendance at this memorial because he
wanted to lure Reacher. He believed Reacher would try to kill
him. He made himself a human target. Then his bodyguards
would kill Reacher. His purpose was to exact revenge on
Reacher."

Gaspar didn't argue. Suicide by cop. Maybe a bit pedestrian
for a Machiavelli like Weston, but not a rare motive among those
angry and feeling persecuted by law enforcement.

"Weston planned to kill Reacher for sixteen years. Don't you
think that's bizarre?" she asked.

"I do." No real reason to argue. Cold revenge and all that.
Besides, he was hungry and didn't want to prolong the
discussion. He rolled the window down, got a good whiff of the
exposed plankton at low tide, and promptly filled the hole with
glass again.

Otto's speculation started next.

"The Boss knew of Weston's plan and thought it might
work," she said. "He knew Reacher could show up. The
memorial was well publicized. Reacher might have learned
about it, depending on where the hell he's hiding at the moment.
The Boss knew we could get caught in the crossfire."

Gaspar shrugged. "Probably."

"You don't care?" she asked, pugnaciously as usual.

He could feel her anguish, but none of his own. He had no
illusions about their Boss. This assignment had almost killed
them both more than once already. Why should today be
different?

"Doesn't matter whether I care or not, Sunshine."

Her shoulders slumped as her steely defiance melted. "He
knew, and sent us in anyway," she said. "That's the worst part."

"It is what it is. You know that. Stop expecting him to

change." Gaspar had twenty years to go and no alternative career he could fathom. But Otto was ambitious. She had plans. Options. She should move on before this assignment got her killed or ruined her life, whichever came first. She should have moved on already. But he knew she wouldn't. So he said nothing more.

After a couple of seconds of silence emphasizing Otto's malaise passed between them, she asked, "Did you see Reacher anywhere?"

Gaspar remembered the glint in the sniper's nest, but wagged his head. "Weston's delusional. So's the Boss."

She seemed to feel slightly better when he voiced what amounted to confirmation that Otto hadn't been derelict somehow and missed Reacher when he was right there, larger than life.

Gaspar said, "Our flight's at midnight. We've got maybe four hours left to kill before we're stuck here. We can have a decent dinner, find out what that reporter knows about Reacher, go back to the hospital for Weston's statement, and then head out."

When she didn't reply, he said, "You're such a foodie. I figured you'd be thrilled about our dining experience, Susie Wong. You're in for a treat."

"It's about time you took me to a decent joint, Chico," she replied, a small grin lifting the corners of her lips.

Which was also true. So Gaspar laughed and he felt good when she joined in, for once.

CHAPTER TWELVE

BEFORE THE TRAFFIC LIGHT at the intersection of Bayshore and Gandy Boulevard, Carson's convertible pulled into the left turn lane and stopped briefly before crossing the eastbound traffic lanes to reach the Plant Key Bridge. A simple two-lane track lying flat above the shallow Hillsborough Bay. One way on and one way off the private island. Which was probably both the good news and the bad news, depending on the traffic and whether one was inclined to feel trapped.

Carson rushed into the surprisingly crowded parking lot at the front entrance.

The red brick building fairly twinkled in the gathering dark. Indoor lighting spilled cheerfully through the windows. The rest of the place was bathed by floodlights around the perimeter. Smaller light streams punctuated the darkness and the steel minaret on the roof.

Gaspar lost track of Carson and Kimball while he searched for an open parking space.

"This place is amazing," Otto said.

"What? Doesn't your Michigan house look exactly like that?"

"I thought it looked familiar," she said, which made him feel better. She'd emerged from her mood, at least.

"First time I came here," he said, "I was told the place was built as a private home. Can you imagine living in a place like this? Servants and horses and such, of course."

"Pretty idyllic setting for a restaurant, too," she replied, still taking everything in. "Now I really feel underdressed."

By the time he settled the sedan appropriately, Carson and Kimball must have already entered the building. Gaspar stopped to stretch when he got out of the sedan, like always. He acted like he was just being lazy. But the truth was that if he didn't stretch out his right leg, he'd fall flat on his face when he tried to move.

Otto watched and waited. "Kimball says she knows everything about the murder of Weston's family. Since Reacher was the investigating officer at the time, she may have some Intel or maybe a couple of leads helpful to us. Let's be sure we don't leave here without it, okay?"

"I'm driving. Can't drink. So I won't have anything better to do," Gaspar said and then set off at as quick a pace as he could manage. But Otto kept up easily. Which was how he judged himself and knew he was moving at glacial speed.

CHAPTER THIRTEEN

KIMBALL WAS WAITING AT the hostess station inside the front entrance. "Judge Carson said she'd be right back and we should look for a booth in the Sunset Bar."

"Lead the way," Gaspar said. He'd been inside the building before, but its old-world charm was no less impressive this time. Spanish influence was heavy, dark, massive, and spacious. He imagined gaslights and servants roaming the halls. Maybe his ancestors had served in such a place in Cuba.

The Sunset Bar was a much more casual eatery than Gaspar expected. A television, booths, a well-stocked bar that hugged the entire side of the room opposite the west-facing windows. Gaspar imagined magnificent sunsets could be enjoyed nightly.

Against all odds, there was one empty booth. The bad news: it was surrounded by listening ears and watching eyes. Which meant less opportunity for intelligence-gathering than Gaspar had hoped.

Kimball slid across the bench and Gaspar settled in next to her on the outside so he would have more room to stretch his right leg unobtrusively. Otto probably noticed. She noticed everything. She slid across the bench on the opposite side facing Kimball and leaving room for Carson opposite Gaspar.

Kimball leaned in and said quietly, "Those two guys over there?" She tilted her head to her right, indicating which ones she meant. "They get around. I saw them at the memorial service today. I noticed because they were also at the execution of the killer of Weston's family. A third guy was with them both times."

Impressive memory, Gaspar thought. Probably came in handy for a reporter.

Both men were Weston's age. Latin. Heavy-set. Casually and expensively dressed. They didn't look exactly like mobsters, but they weren't ordinary businessmen having an after work drink, either.

Otto was sitting upright now. In a conversational tone, she asked, "Do you know who they are?"

"That's one of the things on my list to find out."

"What did the third guy look like?" Gaspar asked, although he suspected he already knew.

"Like he'd been to hell and didn't make it back. What you'd notice about him first was a black eye patch covering an empty eye socket. Scars from a healed head injury." She hesitated a second. "Something wrong with one of his hands, too, but I didn't see it well enough to describe."

"That sounds like the fellow who shot Weston this morning. What did Crane say his name was?" Gaspar searched his memory for the name but before it came up, Otto supplied it.

"Michael Vernon."

Kimball nodded slowly as if she was searching her internal hard drive for data on Vernon and coming up empty. Which Gaspar figured was a ruse of some sort. Surely she'd found a way to get a look at the shooter earlier today. If so, she'd have already made this connection. Not that she owed him anything, but what other information was she holding back?

A waiter appeared at the table with menus and took drink orders. All three ordered coffee. Kimball and Otto ordered black. Gaspar requested *café con leche*, the rich, Cuban coffee heavily laced with heated milk.

"What's the best dinner on the menu?" Otto asked.

"You can't go wrong," the waiter replied. "George's Place has the best chefs in the city. The food here in the Sunset Bar is the same you'd get in the dining room."

Otto said, "What did you have for dinner?"

He grinned. "My favorite is the Thomas Jefferson Roast Beef. Hands down."

"I'll have that," Otto said, handing the menu back.

"I'd add the pear salad with gorgonzola," he said.

"Sold."

"Make it two," Kimball said.

"Three," Gaspar said.

"You got it," the waiter replied, before collecting their menus. "Be right back with the coffee while you wait."

When they were alone again, Kimball said, "Like you, I'm handicapped a bit because I don't know Tampa all that well. We can ask Judge Carson who those guys are. She might know, if they're regulars. Or if she doesn't, she can find out, since her husband owns the place."

Otto's eyes popped open a little wider, but Kimball had been watching her quarry and didn't notice.

Gaspar played white knight for Otto and pupil for Kimball at the same time. "I didn't know Carson's husband owned this restaurant. His name must be George?"

Kimball returned her gaze to Gaspar and Otto and her lips turned up in the most natural grin Gaspar had seen from her yet. She had a pretty face when she wasn't scowling. Which had been rarely so far.

"Let's give the Cuban dude a cigar," she said. "Speaking of which, Willa Carson smokes Cuban cigars. You probably didn't know that, either, did you?"

This time, Gaspar did laugh out loud. The flamboyant Judge Willa Carson was becoming more and more interesting. Too bad he wasn't posted to the FBI's Tampa field office. Sounded like a lot more fun than Miami.

"I'll be sure to ask her if she'd like an after-dinner smoke if we have the time." Cuban cigars were illegal, but the tobacco was now being grown in places like the Dominican Republic. The best ones were hand-rolled, of course, and aged until just the right flavor was to be experienced. Gaspar hadn't enjoyed a quality cigar since he left Miami and he missed them.

He'd have asked more questions, but Otto interrupted the foolishness. "So those two guys and the shooter killed today must be locals. These two must also know Weston. Might have known the Weston family shooter, too, if they got permission to attend his execution."

Kimball said, "Makes sense to me."

"So whatever connection all five men have must relate back in time, at least, to the murder of Weston's family," Otto continued.

If you didn't know her, you'd think she was simply musing out loud. But she'd already reached conclusions and was just polishing them.

Gaspar said nothing.

"Makes sense," Kimball replied. "I can't confirm that, based on my investigation so far, but it's a good working hypothesis and probably true. You're FBI agents. You could ask them. It's illegal to lie to a federal agent."

"You said Weston owed money to a gang that he didn't pay," Otto said. "You said that's why his family was killed."

"Yes."

"What kind of gang? Drugs? Human trafficking?"

Kimball shook her head. "The gang itself was probably involved in all of that. But Weston's vice was gambling. Got in way over his head, as gamblers often do."

"Back then, when Weston's family was murdered, gambling was mostly illegal here except for Greyhound racing," Gaspar supplied for Otto's benefit.

"Dog racing?" Otto said. "There's that much money involved in dog racing?"

"I guess there could be," Kimball said. "But Weston's gambling was the illegal kind. The allegations that Reacher investigated at the time involved pari-mutuel betting."

"OTB," Gaspar explained. "Off track betting. Down in the Miami office, we've got several OTB joints on our constant watch list. It's legal and regulated these days. In Florida, OTB is a money maker for the state. But it's also a cesspool of corruption where a guy with a gambling problem can get into really big trouble."

"Exactly. Weston got in way over his head. He was employed by Uncle Sam in a military job that, well, let's just say it didn't pay a million a year."

"He owed a million bucks?" Gaspar asked.

Kimball nodded. "He had no way to come up with that kind of money. He was a high-profile guy here and the gang decided to make an example of him. They told him to pay up or his family would pay for him. Apparently, he chose option two. Scumbag."

Kimball stopped talking while the waiter delivered the coffee.

When he left, Otto said, "You're saying Reacher discovered all of that and arrested Weston, but the locals couldn't prove any of it? So Weston walked away?"

Gaspar thought that sounded exactly like Reacher's methods. He'd have figured everything out and handled the matter himself. He didn't worry much about whether the courts accepted his proof.

Kimball sipped her coffee and returned Otto's level gaze. "That's how it looks from the file and everything else I've found. Weston didn't pull the trigger, but he didn't do anything to stop the killing, either. Of course he denied all involvement. He had an alibi. The shooter confessed. There was no evidence of Weston's debt. No evidence that the threat had been made by the gang or ignored by Weston. The gang leader certainly didn't come forward."

"No admissible evidence against Weston, so he was released. And Reacher was already gone by the time everything was sorted out."

As Otto completed her sentence, the fourth member of their dinner party arrived and slid into the booth across from Gaspar.

"From Weston's questions at the hospital, I gather your assignment has something to do with Jack Reacher," Carson said as she waved to the waiter to let him know we were all collected. Seeing they were drinking coffee, she ordered *café con leche* for herself and picked up the menu for a quick look. Gaspar figured she had to have it memorized by now. "I met him once when he was here."

"You met who?" Otto asked.

"Who was here?" Kimball asked simultaneously.

Carson decided on dinner, put the menu down, and glanced at Otto and Kimball. "Jack Reacher. He didn't stay long. But I'm told he never does."

The waiter took her order and refilled the coffee. He was even more attentive now that the boss's wife was in the house.

"What was Reacher doing here?" Otto asked, after the waiter left.

Carson settled back into the booth and turned slightly so she was facing everyone. She seemed to make a few quick decisions before she answered. "This is not my case. If it were, I wouldn't be discussing this with you. I'm on call tonight and that's the only reason I agreed to preside over the two sworn statements."

Gaspar figured she was splitting hairs for reasons of her own. But Weston was not his concern and Reacher was. He didn't care about her legal balancing act, but he was impressed with the way she slid around the rules without breaking any.

Otto, ever the lawyer, replied, "Understood." Maybe she felt the same way Gaspar did. "We're doing a routine background check on Reacher for the special personnel task force. Anything you can tell us about him would be helpful."

"I looked into the files today when the FBI asked me to preside over Weston's statement and saw that Reacher was here in the late summer of 1997."

A few months after Weston's family was murdered, Gaspar calculated. Also after the killer was arrested and Weston released. About six months after Reacher left the Army, too. He'd failed to get Weston for the murders the first time. His bulldog tenacity must have pulled him back again for another try after his Army discharge, long after he should have moved on.

"I remembered meeting him. He's not the kind of guy you're likely to forget," Carson said. "Weston ended up in Tampa Southern Hospital almost dead that time, too."

"Which explains why Weston didn't attend the first annual memorial service once he was released from jail after his family was killed. And after that, he's been out of the country," Kimball voiced the thought that had occurred simultaneously to Gaspar.

The food was delivered. Carson and Kimball fell on the meal like feral dogs, but Otto ignored her food, focused on Reacher like a heat-seeking missile. Gaspar felt his stomach growling, but felt he should hold back until Otto tucked.

Carson gestured toward the plates. "We don't have a lot of time. We can talk and eat simultaneously. I've done it for years."

Otto lifted her fork and Gaspar dug in as if he hadn't had a decent meal in weeks. Which he hadn't. The food was amazing, even better than he remembered. Exactly the sort of meal his wife loved. The beef was rare and crusted with mango chutney. The Madeira mushroom sauce was light but flavorful. The combination of ripe Bartlett pears, Gorgonzola cheese, candied walnuts and vinaigrette perfectly blended. A dry Cabernet would have made the meal one of his wife's all-time top five. Which meant he couldn't tell her about it. At least, not until he could bring her to experience the meal herself.

"We've never met Reacher," Otto said, barely moving her fork around the ambrosia on her plate. "What's he like?"

"Big. Quiet. No fashion sense at all," Carson laughed. When Otto didn't grin, Carson seemed to consider the question more seriously. Slowly, as if she was uncovering buried artifacts from the depths of memory, she said, "He stood out like a sore thumb, but he exuded confidence like a force field that repelled all challengers. He seemed American, but not American at the same time. In the way that military kids do. Like he held a valid passport but didn't really belong here. He didn't seem to care that he didn't belong. He didn't seem to care about much of anything, actually."

"Was he living in Tampa? Or visiting someone?" Kimball asked. Maybe she was thinking about the gambling situation. Or maybe she thought Reacher was looking for Weston, too.

"He said he was passing through. He asked me where the bus station was. Headed north, I think. Atlanta, maybe?" She wiped the Madeira sauce off her mouth with her napkin and sat back from her plate. "Of course, everywhere in the country is north of here, and most roads lead to Atlanta."

Kimball said, "From what you've described, Reacher doesn't seem like the kind of guy you'd even come into contact with, Judge. Where'd you meet him?"

"Didn't I start with that? Sorry. A fundraiser. We attend dozens of those things. This one was education scholarships for military orphans, I think."

"Where was the event held? At MacDill?"

"Greyhound Lanes," Carson replied. She must have noticed their bewilderment. "Not the bus station or a bowling alley. The dog track."

"Dog racing?"

"Yes. Why?"

"Was Weston there?"

"If he was an officer at MacDill then, he might have attended the fundraiser. Sure. Quite a few military folks were there. It's a big annual event. Very popular. Huge family affair."

Kimball looked toward the two Latin kings across the room. "Anything to do with those guys sitting over there? They look familiar to me, but I can't place them."

Carson turned around to check. "That's Alberto and Franco Vernon. They might have been at the fundraiser. They're not involved with Greyhound Lanes. But they do own a pari-mutuel track a few miles north of here."

"Are they related to Michael Vernon?" Kimball asked, naming the dead man Agent Crane had identified as today's shooter.

Carson set her fork on her plate briefly, composing her reply with care because the question came too close to the case she was handling. "They have a brother named Michael, yes. Theirs is a large local family. Long-time Tampa businesspeople. Significant contributors to the community. Like most large families, some members are more successful than others. But they're protective of their own."

Gaspar received the definite message that no further questions would be entertained about the Vernons. Kimball must have received the same message because she didn't press further. After a few moments, Carson picked up her fork and resumed her meal at a slower pace.

Otto, fixated as ever, asked, "Did Reacher say why he was there? At the fundraiser?"

"If he did, I don't recall. But I'd doubt it. He didn't say much of anything. Not a conversationalist, let's put it that way." Carson glanced at the television mounted on the wall above the bar in the corner. "We're out of time. Let's finish up our food and head back. Agent Crane will report me to the chief judge if we're any later."

The way she grinned made Gaspar feel there was a story there about her relationship with the chief judge she wasn't sharing. Which was too bad. Because it was probably one he'd enjoy.

CHAPTER FOURTEEN

OTTO AND GASPAR ARRIVED at the hospital's main entrance first. They signed in again at the information desk and wandered through the maze of some administrator's idea of organized healthcare. Eventually, they located the OR waiting room where they had agreed to rejoin the others two hours ago. Nightfall came early in November, but the view from the waiting room window was no less appealing, Gaspar noticed. Bright moonlight and illumination along Bayshore Boulevard rendered it more magical than in daylight, not less.

Agents Crane and Bartos were seated with open briefcases on their laps amid candy bar wrappers and empty paper coffee cups.

"Looks like you guys enjoyed a gourmet supper, too," Gaspar said.

Crane just glowered at him.

"Where's Jennifer Lane?" Gaspar asked.

Bartos replied, "Samantha Weston asked for her about five minutes ago. As soon as Judge Carson and the court reporter get here, we'll all go back in there and finish up and get out of here."

As if his words had conjured her, Carson opened the door and said, "Ms. Chernow texted me on our way back. She says she's setting up. Let's get this done so these patients can get some rest."

They all started after her down the hallway toward the recovery room where they had left both Westons.

After less than twenty feet of progress, everything went to hell.

First, the unmistakable sound of two quick gunshots filled the quiet corridor. A woman screamed. Another woman shouted words Gaspar could not make out. And two more quick gunshots followed.

Otto pulled her Sig Sauer and ran forward, ahead of Gaspar. He pulled his Glock and followed close behind.

Weapons drawn, Crane and Bartos brought up the rear.

Before they reached the room, he heard another gunshot.

Willa Carson ran past them back toward the staircase. An instant later, a horrifically loud buzzing sound exploded around them. She'd pulled the fire alarm. When Gaspar glanced back past the other two agents, he saw the Judge had grabbed her cell phone and was already dialing.

The narrow, hospital-paraphernalia-choked corridor left the agents no choice but to charge single file toward the source of the gunshots.

Just before Otto reached the recovery room doorway, Natalie Chernow dashed out and crashed into her. Otto pushed her against the wall and tried to ask what had happened, but she was sobbing and babbling incomprehensibly. Not that she could've been heard over the alarm in any case, much less over the sirens outside that now joined the cacophony. The din was deafening.

Gaspar supposed he should take comfort in the rapid

response rate by everyone involved, but there was no time to appreciate that just then. Otto shoved the court reporter to him and he passed her back to the agents behind him, then followed Otto into the room where he could just hear her shouting "FBI! FBI" over the pandemonium. Sound reverberated through Gaspar's entire body like electroshock.

CHAPTER FIFTEEN

THE FIRST PERSON GASPAR saw was Jennifer Lane.

She stood empty-handed, staring, eyes as wide as basketballs.

The deafening fire alarm continued, now transitioned to incessant blasts brief moments apart, loud enough to wake the morgue.

Just ahead of him, he saw Otto pivot, assume shooter stance and yell, "Hands up! Hands up!"

Steven Kent stood facing Otto, one hand extended with a .38 caliber handgun pointed toward Jennifer Lane.

Slowly, he raised both hands in the air. He pointed the gun in his right hand toward the ceiling. His blue scrubs, face, arms, and hands were splattered with blood. But he made no further move. He said nothing. He seemed to understand what was expected of a man in his situation and he performed appropriately.

Like the pause button on a video had been pushed, all action stopped for a long moment, and then each actor in the drama flew into perfectly scripted motion.

Agents Crane and Bartos quickly controlled the shooter. Otto confirmed both Westons were dead.

Gaspar approached Jennifer Lane, who stared as if the scene remained paused at a point when Kent had shot both Westons twice in the head, shot and missed Natalie Chernow, and turned the gun on her.

"Ms. Lane," Gaspar said, grasping her elbow. "Jennifer? It's okay. Are you hurt?" She did not answer. Her face was pale. She was breathing rapidly. Pupils were dilated. The skin of her arm was cold and clammy to his touch.

"Come over here," he said, but the accursed fire alarm continued and he had to shout to be heard. He holstered his weapon and tried to lead her away from the carnage, but her terror acted like adhesive on her soles. She would not move.

Gaspar yelled, "Jennifer! Jennifer!"

Finally, she turned her head to look at him, but she didn't see him. He could tell. Grasping her arm again as gently as he could, he again tried to lead her away. But she wouldn't budge.

She returned her stare toward the bloody mess that had been Samantha Weston.

Gaspar tried once more to get through to her. He shook her a little bit and yelled to be heard over the damned obnoxious buzzing of the fire alarm.

"Jennifer! Let's go!" She didn't move.

Then instantly the fire alarm stopped. Its absence was surreal, and the unnerving quiet acted like a switch to release Jenny from horrified rigidity. Before he could do more than slow her descent with his grip on her elbow, she fainted and collapsed into a pile on the shiny waxed floor.

In the eerie silence, Gaspar could hear Crane repeating the familiar words accompanying arrest, including full Miranda warnings. Bartos had collected Kent's gun and was using his cell phone to call for backup.

Otto asked Kent, "Steven what were you thinking? Why did you do this?"

Kent said nothing, which Kent had the presence of mind to know was absolutely the best thing to do under the circumstances.

Agent Crane led Stephen Kent toward the exit.

CHAPTER SIXTEEN

ON THE INSTRUCTIONS OF one of the other agents, Kimball had been standing inside the recovery room blocking the door to prevent anyone from entering. She moved aside for Crane and Bartos to lead Kent away, then pulled the door closed behind them and approached Gaspar.

"Let's get Jenny into the waiting room. We can talk there."

Gaspar saw Otto making use of the small window of calm before the room crawled with crime scene personnel to capture evidence of the murders with her smart phone. She'd find him when she was finished.

For the first time, Gaspar noticed the citrus scent mingling with the metallic odor of blood and disinfectants.

When he looked again at Jenny Lane's pale face, eyes closed, barely breathing in a heap on the polished floor, Gaspar realized why she'd seemed so familiar. She looked ghostly like the victim in a missing person's case he'd assisted for the Tampa FBI detail with some follow up in Miami. The two could have been sisters, even. That victim had disappeared from her home and he'd never heard what happened to her. But her name wasn't Jennifer Lane.

He shrugged. He'd seen look-a-likes before. But he felt better that he'd finally made the memory connection.

Kimball collected Jenny Lane's things from the chair and helped him lift her from the floor. He couldn't carry her. He could barely support his own weight. But with Kimball's help, they were able to move Lane into the corridor.

Agent Bartos stood guard outside the recovery room to secure the crime scene until appropriate crews arrived. In the corridor, the business of a quiet hospital floor between surgeries was returning to normal as hospital security calmed patients and personnel. Soon, a different sort of chaos would ensue as the crime scene was processed.

Gaspar and Otto would escape before then.

CHAPTER SEVENTEEN

THE OR WAITING ROOM would no doubt become command central for the remainder of the night as the scene was processed. For now, the room was available. Gaspar and Kimball half carried, half walked Lane down the hallway.

Willa Carson stood by the door and allowed them to get Jenny settled inside. Ms. Chernow was there composing herself as well.

"Can I have a word with you?" Kimball asked Gaspar. He followed her to a quiet corner. "You're not supposed to be here, are you? Your work is confidential, isn't it?"

He didn't confirm or deny, but her powers of observation hadn't failed her.

"You and Otto should get out while it's still possible. I'll stay here with them and if we find out anything else, I can let you know."

She was right. They needed to go. If Otto didn't show up quickly, they'd be stuck here too long answering too many questions in direct contravention of their orders. The Boss wouldn't like it. But more importantly, he might not be able to erase them from the crime scene once official reporting began.

"Why do you think he did it?" Gaspar asked.

"Why did Kent kill both Westons using the same technique the shooter used to kill Weston's family?" Kimball replied. "Or why did Weston offer himself as a human sacrifice to kill Reacher?"

"Both, I guess."

She shrugged. "Who knows?"

"What's your best guess? That's a place to start."

"The first attack on Weston today was pretty straightforward. Weston was a cat with nine lives. Michael Vernon, the poor dead veteran who tried to kill him, had to be a guy Weston screwed over, like Agent Crane said."

"Makes sense."

"From there, though, it gets tangled. Like I told you, Jenny Lane said Samantha had filed for divorce and offered to testify against her husband to save as much as possible of her assets. Probably a ploy to keep herself out of jail, too."

"Did Lane share any of that testimony with you?" Gaspar asked.

"Not yet. Tangle number two: Weston got a death sentence when he was diagnosed with advanced small cell lung cancer a few weeks ago." Gaspar knew of the cancer, but let her talk. It was almost always a good idea to let people talk themselves out. "Untreatable. He was living on borrowed time. If he'd been conscious when they brought him in here this afternoon, he'd probably have refused those surgeries. It's a miracle he survived them."

"What's your theory on Kent? Why the hell would he do it? Weston was loony enough to hire his own hit just in case Reacher failed to kill him."

"Lung cancer is a nasty way to die," Kimball pointed out.

"Weston was a soldier. He would have preferred a quick bullet to the head."

"And then he finds out his wife is about to betray him, so he orders up a two-for-one hit?"

Kimball nodded. "I got about that far down that rabbit hole, myself," she said. "But then—"

"What self-respecting hit man would do his work, then just stand there and let himself be taken into custody?"

Kimball nodded. "Exactly. Not much of a business model. Unless that was part of the deal. Because that's effectively what the first shooter did, too. He left the Weston house, but he was easy to find."

"Or it could have been bad timing. Maybe Kent thought he'd have time to get away and we returned too soon," Gaspar sighed. "Either way, it leaves us nowhere that makes any sense."

"I wish that were true," Kimball said, her mouth had pressed into a grim line. "Because now I'm thinking I dropped the ball."

"How do you figure?"

"I should've remembered."

"Remembered what?"

"Weston's first wife. Meredith Kent Weston. She was Steven Kent's sister."

So it could have gone either way. Vengeance or contract. Gaspar had stopped trying to find logic in criminal behavior long ago. Life wasn't like fiction. Most of the time, he never learned why. Not that it mattered, really. Weston and his wife were just as dead either way.

CHAPTER EIGHTEEN

TAMPA INTERNATIONAL AIRPORT HAD to be one of the
easiest airports in the country. Returning the sedan was quick
and simple. Security lines were short. For once, they were at the
gate without having to run.

Gaspar figured none of this was good news to Otto. She
hated flying. The process went better when she didn't have time
to change her mind about boarding.

The seats in the gate area were standard black and silver
sling seats. Knockoffs of a contemporary design that most
normal people had never heard of. All filled with tourists and
kids and wrinklies headed in or out of the Sunshine state to avoid
winter weather or celebrate Thanksgiving.

Otto seemed unusually preoccupied, even for her. She had
her laptop open, her smart phone at her ear. She'd checked in
with the Boss. Working. Always working.

She was number one. He was number two. He was only
mildly surprised to realize now that he liked it that way.

Gaspar stretched out, folded his hands over his flat stomach, and
closed his eyes. He had about thirty minutes to doze. A rare gift.

Otto pushed his arm to wake him up from sweet oblivion ten minutes later.

"What?" he said, not opening his eyes.

"Kimball sent me a file. Take a look," she said.

He glanced over to her laptop screen. Two photos. Each of a brown envelope. One larger than the other.

The larger was hand addressed in block printing to Samantha Weston, c/o Jennifer Lane, Esq. The postmark was Washington, D.C. ten days ago. No return address. Apparently, the large envelope had contained the smaller one.

The smaller envelope looked a little worse for age and wear. Dirty smudges around the edges of a square about the size of a deck of playing cards suggested its contents. Black letters that looked like printing on a police report were placed across the flap to show they were written after the envelope was sealed.

Thomas Weston Recorded Statement

10:04 p.m. 9/1997

The envelope's seal had been broken.

Otto scrolled up the screen to the email from Kimball. The subject line was *Received tonight from J.L.*

Gaspar said, "Kimball said Lane had offered to share Samantha Weston's evidence against her husband. That must be it."

Because Otto would have already noticed, he didn't mention the handwriting on both envelopes looked like Reacher's. They'd seen several examples from his old case files where he printed the same way.

Otto nodded. "Kimball attached an audio file of the contents of the cassette tape in the envelope. I've listened to it. It's a full confession. Definitely from Weston in his own voice. He admits everything Reacher said at the time about how and why Weston's family was killed. And a little bit more."

"Such as?"

"Two big things. He and Samantha were having an affair at the time of the murders. And Weston knew the gang would kill his family, but he put everything in place and then just let it happen. Like a kid choosing to let his dog sleep in the middle of the road, even though he knows he's bound to get run over. He knew they were going to die. He simply didn't know when."

"So you figure Kent found all of this out somehow and that's why he killed them both today when he had the chance?" Gaspar asked.

"I don't have to figure anything. I know he found out today, because Weston told him. Jennifer Lane was right there."

"Weston's plan to get Reacher was a bit more clever than we realized, I guess. He had a Plan B if the suicide by Reacher didn't work at the memorial service." Gaspar resettled himself in his chair and nodded at Otto to go on.

"Weston was defeated," she said. "But he had one last chance. When they loaded him into the ambulance at MacDill, he asked to be transported to Tampa Southern. And he asked for Steven Kent, too. Kent told me it was because he had the necessary clearances. But like you said, what clearances would he need to care for an ex-officer?"

"Weston asked for Kent because he knew him. I can buy that," Gaspar said.

"All Weston had to do was point Kent and let him fire, and make sure Samantha went down with him. He manipulated Kent by telling him what was on that recorded statement and demanding that Jennifer Lane play it."

Gaspar wasn't sure all of this held water, but most of it was plausible. And he didn't want to spend his next twenty minutes arguing with her. Weston wasn't their case. Never had been.

He closed his eyes again. "Good to know. But I never doubted Reacher's evidence against Weston anyway. Did you?"

"That's not the most interesting part though," she replied.

He felt her place one of her earbuds to his ear and turn up the volume on the recording. "This was on the end of the Weston taped confession."

For the first time, relaxed in the Tampa airport, eyes closed, almost asleep, Gaspar heard Reacher speak. It had to be him.

The voice wasn't what he'd expected. Range was higher, for one thing. Tenor, not bass. Speech clipped. Accent sort of nondescript Midwest American. If Gaspar had been pressed to describe it to another officer, he'd have said Reacher sounded less dangerous than he knew him to be. Maybe that's how he got close to his targets.

The words were about what Gaspar had guessed, though.

Reacher said, "You got lucky, Weston. You ever step out of line again your whole miserable life, I'll find you. And I'll make you sorry. Count on it."

Gaspar felt his lips turn up of their own accord as he wondered whether Kent had pulled the trigger on that .38 this afternoon at all.

THE END

MISTAKEN
JUSTICE

For Evelyn

CHAPTER ONE

WICKED COLD RAIN BLACKENED the night outside the small country house near Plant City while brilliant light and celebration reigned inside. Noisemakers, balloons, and spiked punch encouraged merriment, but Darla Nixon was isolated from the party both by the throbbing headache between her brows and because she was the boss. Not just another member of the team, she was the principal, responsible for everything about Abraham Lincoln Elementary. She felt her responsibilities keenly. And she loved her work.

When she closed her eyes briefly, her eyelids scraped like Brillo. She winced at the burn. A soothing tear escaped each eye. Exhaustion claimed her.

How long had it been since she'd slept? More than the routine insomnia she'd learned to cope with, her failure to rest over the busy holiday season had finally caught up with her. Darla craved the silence of the rain-soaked night, imagining it might soothe her to sleep.

A comforting hand rested on her shoulder. Darla opened her eyes to gaze into Marie Webster's concerned face. The young woman was holding a glass of something stronger than spiked punch; the glow on her face was more than pride.

"Are you feeling okay?"

Darla smiled gently, laying her hand over Marie's. The younger woman's selection as *Teacher of the Year* had come as no surprise to her principal. Darla envied the kindergarten students who flourished under Marie's nurturing, comfortable style. Many days, Darla wished *she* could sit in Marie's lap and enjoy chocolate milk and gingerbread cookies, too.

"Is it your eyes?"

The tightly-controlled Marie didn't drink often. Her words slurred around before they emerged too slowly. Darla didn't mind. Marie was entitled to some fun; there was precious little of it in her life.

Marie's query referred to the retinitis pigmentosa that was destroying Darla's eyesight, marching forward relentlessly, blocking the light until ultimately she'd be blind. The day was coming. Darla had been staving it off for twenty years but she knew her luck would run out. Most RP patients were legally blind by 40, and Darla was more than ten years beyond that. She lived on borrowed light.

At her eye exam two months ago, the specialist had confirmed the blind spots in her visual fields that Darla concealed from everyone else.

"You must give up driving, Darla. Especially at night," he'd told her, noting his recommendations in his chart as he talked. "You have almost no peripheral vision on the right side and your night vision is extremely poor now. Driving is too dangerous. For you, and for everyone else on the road."

She'd told no one about the results of those tests, nor did she intend to. She couldn't give up driving. Since her two sons left home for college six years ago Darla had lived alone. She took care of herself, drove to work and back, did her own food shopping and preparation. She would not give up her independence. Her old car had so many dents from her various misjudgments, Darla had stopped noticing them. No, she would continue to do what she'd done the past three years: drive as little as possible and hope for the best.

Now, Darla patted Marie's hand again. "I'm feeling a little tired. Would you mind if I didn't stay for the cake?"

"Of course not. I'd offer to drive you home, but I'm a bit tipsy."

Before Marie's words were spoken, Darla refused. The last thing she wanted was to spoil the party and draw attention to her condition. She suspected that her team would really cut loose once the boss was gone, and that was perfectly okay. They worked hard. They deserved to celebrate.

"Well, at least, let me see you out, then," Marie's selfless compassion seemed limitless, despite her own personal challenges. Marie handled her life as a single mother of a mentally-handicapped eight-year-old son with such aplomb. Oh, many times Darla had been the one to console Marie. Paul could be quite a handful. He acted out often, more like an irritable two-year-old than a child his age.

Paul had several medical problems and he was often mistreated by other children. Such inevitable events of childhood were especially cruel to the young woman and her hopelessly immature son. Still, Darla suspected Marie was stronger than she, even if Marie didn't realize it.

Darla glanced up at the banner over the kitchen table. *Teacher of the Year*. Darla was proud of Marie, of all she'd overcome, of all she'd managed to accomplish. But she knew

Marie had a tough road ahead, too. Paul's mental capacity would not improve, but he would grow taller and stronger. His uncontrollable rages would become impossible for Marie to manage on her own. They'd discussed all of this before, and Darla had asked for legal advice about Marie's options from her friend, Judge Willa Carson. Darla planned to persuade Marie with Willa's help, but Darla said nothing more tonight. A party wasn't the time or place for serious conversations.

Darla patted Marie's shoulder saying, "Congratulations, honey."

Marie replied, "I couldn't have done it without you. You believed in me when no one else did. You've helped me so much with Paul. I can't thank you enough, Darla. Really."

"Where is Paul tonight?" Darla asked as they walked to the door. She watched Marie's expression anxiously. The child meant everything to his mother, a situation destined to bring heartache.

"He's staying overnight with a neighbor's boy. It's the first night I've had to myself in years." Marie placed Darla's sweater over her shoulders, opened the door, and held the umbrella over their heads while they walked across the muddy yard to Darla's car.

"Are you sure that's a good idea?"

"Don't worry so much," Marie chastised her gently. "Paul's played over there before. I think it'll be all right. If not, I guess Ginny will call me and I'll go pick him up."

When Darla was safely inside, Marie leaned into the front seat and said, "Watch those trash bags out there. This wind is likely to have blown them into the street. Pickup isn't until tomorrow." Marie closed the car door firmly and stood looking into the window.

Darla started the car, turned on the lights, flipped the windshield wipers to high and waited. The wind blew hard, cold rain across the driveway, pushing Marie to hurry back to the house, unsteady on her feet. She waved to Darla from the doorway until something inside captured her attention. Marie closed the door firmly, extinguishing the stream of light that had brightened the sidewalk, plunging Darla into almost total darkness. Only her headlights dimly illuminated the yard. She shivered.

"No time like the present," Darla said aloud, took a deep breath, pressed her foot on the brake pedal and shifted into reverse.

CHAPTER TWO

NO STREET LIGHTS LINED the country road. Darla glanced back toward the decrepit home once more. Marie could barely afford to pay the rent on this old place. Darla worried about the kinds of neighbors that surrounded Paul here. The area housed thugs and thieves who committed violent crimes almost daily.

She scolded herself. "Marie is just one of thirty teachers at school. The principal can't handle the personal problems of all of them."

But she wanted to take care of them all. Marie's situation pierced her heart more than some of the others, although Darla felt responsible for each of her teachers. All of the students, too.

"Well, quit stalling. It's not going to get any better out here," Darla said under her breath. She turned off the radio. Her head was already pounding and only total concentration would help her to drive home in the darkness that consumed the car and everything around her.

She lifted her foot bravely off the brake pedal, backed with care down the driveway and out into the dark street, shifted her shoulders and turned her head as far as possible to the right to peer into the black night.

Once on the road and facing forward, Darla placed the car into gear, pressed the accelerator gently, and cautiously navigated around the potholes in the dirt trail. Her concentration was so fierce she could almost see the rough road ahead in the inky blackness.

Darla pulled around the crater in the middle of her lane, swerved to port and crossed the centerline. Her left front tire fell into a hole the size of Lake Okeechobee and she jerked the wheel too quickly to the right to steer out of it. The car bounced into another pothole, when simultaneously the gale slammed a plastic trash can into the right-front side. A solid but muffled thud added percussion to the slapping windshield wipers and the howling wind.

"Shoot!" Darla swore, grinning when she heard the sanitized epithet acceptable for an elementary school principal. Had she forgotten how to curse, even privately?

The sedan lurched to a brief stop, its right wheel stuck in the deep hole. Darla punched the accelerator to heave out. The wheels caught some traction and the car moved abruptly. She felt a trash bag under the right rear wheel and pressed the accelerator a bit harder, suffering the prolonged, rough bounce of the old seat against the springs.

"What a mess!"

Briefly, Darla considered venturing into the cold rain and cleaning up the raunchy garbage she'd no doubt strewn over the entire road. But fatigue overwhelmed her.

"I'm sorry guys," she said aloud to the county collectors who would have to clean up after her tomorrow. They would no doubt be able to recall many unsuitable names to call a principal who set such a bad example.

Half an hour later Darla reached her small ranch style house in a modest Tampa neighborhood. She parked in the driveway, regretting that she'd never built a garage, or at least a carport. Raising and educating two sons had produced too many expenses and too little cash.

Eschewing the inevitable losing battle between her umbrella and the wind, Darla struggled out of the car, rushed to the side door, and let herself into her home. Fifteen minutes later, she'd taken a sleeping pill, gone to bed, turned out the lights and laid her head gratefully on the down pillow.

The sleeping pill would leave her groggy tomorrow, but tonight she would rest. As she settled into sleep, a small flash of memory teased her subconscious.

She heard the plastic can bomb her vehicle and felt again the rolling motion her seat made as the car's right rear tire passed over the lumpy bag of waste.

Her last thought before chemical oblivion overcame her was that she hoped the garbage she'd strewn over the road was not toxic to animals roaming the countryside that night.

How lucky she'd been that she'd only hit a trashcan and not a dog or a cat.

CHAPTER THREE

DARLA'S SCREAMS AWAKENED HER from nightmares of blindness and dependency. The dreams were always the same: Her RP had progressed. She could discern only dim shapes in a small field of tunnel vision directly in front of her face. She couldn't read or experience her friend's expressions of joy or sorrow. Immersing herself in films or television was impossible. Her hair was disheveled and her lipstick smeared. In the most terrifying night scenes, she lived in a filthy institution where vicious mental patients attacked her and she didn't know who they were or why they hated her so.

Darla knew that blind didn't mean helpless. She realized lack of sight was not a death sentence.

But at night when she was alone, her conscious defenses down, fear overwhelmed her reason. Many mornings, she awakened shaken, sweating and trembling. She didn't need a psychiatrist to tell her the root of her insomnia was her overwhelming fear of the perpetual, unrelenting darkness.

After her shower she felt better. Darla flipped on the television in the kitchen as she pushed the bread down into the toaster and poured coffee into the mug Marie's son, Paul, had given her for Christmas. The mug displayed two stick figures drawn with crayons, one taller, wearing a skirt and the other with short, spiked brown hair. The hand-printed inscription said, "We love you, Darla." Paul had made the drawing himself, but his mother had printed the words. This tangible evidence of Paul's affection for Darla brought tears. On his good days, he could be such a gentle child.

Darla glanced outside. Still raining. The dull gray sky pressed down on the wetness stealing all color from the normally vivid Florida landscape. Wind whipped the palm trees from side to side as if their trunks were rubber. On mornings like this Darla longed to bundle up in her warm bathrobe, drink strong, sweetened coffee with heavy cream and read. She loved reading and she'd lose the ability, too soon. Marie encouraged her to learn Braille. Darla wasn't ready to surrender to that yet.

As if her thoughts had conjured the young teacher, Darla noticed Marie's picture on television, a crowd gathered around her. Where was she? A hospital? Darla turned up the sound.

Rosa Rodriguez, a local reporter, said, "Paul Webster was struck by a hit and run driver last night. Because he was supposed to be spending the night with a neighbor, his mother didn't know he was injured until early this morning when she found him lying on the side of the road. He was airlifted here to Tampa Southern Hospital and remains in intensive care. His condition is listed as critical."

Darla's hand shook as she drew the coffee mug from her mouth and set it on the counter. Paul hurt and in the hospital, lying outside all night in the rain, alone. Her stomach roiled and her legs weakened. She sat heavily onto the chair, stared at the screen, and clasped her hands together to steady them.

She remembered the sickening thud against her car, the lump under the wheels. Surely, a plastic garbage can the wind tossed against her car? She couldn't have hit a *child*? Paul was slight, but he weighed eighty pounds. If she'd hit him, wouldn't she have known it?

Rodriguez turned to the uniformed man standing next to her. "This is Hillsborough County Sheriff's Traffic Homicide Detective Kevin Cook. Detective Cook, can you tell us why you're investigating this traffic accident? Homicide detectives don't normally investigate hit and run vehicle accidents, do they?"

And Paul's not dead, Darla whispered, *Thank God.*

Kevin Cook stood erect, his hands folded in front of him, shoulders broad, eyes staring forward, mouth pressed to judgmental hardness. Detective Kevin Cook had been one of Darla's students long ago. A straight-arrow even then, she was not surprised when he joined the Sheriff's Office after three years of service in the Navy right out of high school. He'd advanced rapidly and had to be one of the youngest detectives on the force. What was he? Twenty-five, maybe thirty? It was hard to keep track of her students, she'd taught so many.

Darla watched him now with a mixture of pride and fear. Detective Kevin Cook would exhaust all leads. Marie could be comforted by faith in his persistent resolve. Darla should expect hot pursuit until every aspect of the crime she'd committed was exposed.

She thought briefly of calling Willa Carson, but rejected the idea immediately. Willa was a friend, but she'd advise Darla to tell the police everything. At the moment, Darla wasn't ready to face the consequences. She could always call Willa later. After she knew more facts.

"Paul Webster is in critical condition. We take the matter very seriously," Detective Cook said, not actually answering the question Rodriguez asked him. Was Paul that close to death, then? Was the Sheriff's office expecting the matter to become a homicide?

"Do you have any information you can share with us about the incident?" Rodriguez asked, seeking a pithy sound bite the local news stations could replay later.

"There is a witness," he said. "A neighbor saw the car strike Paul, although he didn't realize the driver had hit a child at the time. He describes the car as an older model, mid-sized sedan, dark color."

"Oh, my God," Darla whispered. She glanced at her six-year-old navy sedan sitting in the muddy driveway.

"We hear a lot about forensics. Can we expect some dramatic forensic solution to this crime?" Rodriguez suggested.

Kevin frowned. Anger roughened his tone and edged his features. "Rain washed most of the forensic evidence away."

"So you're saying you don't know who hit Paul and you don't think you'll find the driver?" Rodriguez asked.

Detective Cook turned his hard gaze into the camera's lens where he stared directly into Darla's guilty heart.

"Oh, we'll find him," he said. "We won't give up."

Darla dropped her head onto the table and sobbed, tears meant for Paul, Marie and herself.

After awhile she moved to the back door, pulled an umbrella open, and walked out into the storm. She maneuvered around the puddles to the right side of her now monstrous car and stared.

Rain pelted the umbrella without mercy while the wind turned it almost inside out. Cleaner than the car had been in a long time, rain had washed away everything, even the crusty white bird droppings that had adorned the hood and roof for weeks.

Darla knelt down in the mud. She inspected the car's side from the front bumper to the back one. She ran her palm over the cool, wet steel. All the dents she felt had been inflicted a while ago, as far as she could remember. And if there had been, God forbid, blood on the car, it was long gone. No, the hateful sedan appeared just as it had yesterday. Old, worn, dented.

She couldn't have hit a little boy with this car and run over his body and leave no evidence of the carnage. She couldn't have.

Drenched by the driving rain, Darla stood and felt her way back to the house. She stopped under the small, inadequate roof barely covering the back stoop, closed the umbrella and shook off the water as best she could. She turned to stare toward the car once more.

She would never drive it again. The thought offered little comfort.

"Too bad you didn't make that decision yesterday," she scolded herself aloud, in the same tone she used to discipline her worst-behaved students before calling their parents.

Inside, she pulled a different coffee mug out of the cabinet, filled it with strong black coffee, and returned to the television. She shivered in her cold, wet clothes as she checked all of the channels, but heard no further report on Paul's accident.

She clicked her accuser off, laid the remote down, and considered what to do now. Calling Willa Carson was not an option. Willa was a judge, charged with dispensing justice not avoiding it. No. Darla would have to figure something out on her own.

CHAPTER FOUR

TWO HOURS LATER, DARLA willingly paid the taxi driver
who dropped her off at Tampa Southern Hospital's front
entrance. She'd come to support Marie, who had no one else to
console her. Darla was ashamed of herself for her cowardly
delay, particularly since Marie expected her to help. Reliable
Darla provided Marie's safety net, never allowing Marie to fall
too far, too fast, offering the kind of help no one had given Darla
when she could have used it most.

At the information desk, Darla asked, "Where is Intensive
Care?"

"Do you have family in the ICU?" the kindly volunteer
asked.

"Paul Webster. I'm his aunt," Darla lied.

Because she was the only family Marie and Paul had.

Marie's own parents were dead, and Paul's father had
abandoned them years ago when Paul's mental handicap became
undeniable. Paul was about sixteen months old and Marie was an
eighteen-year-old college freshman when she answered Darla's
advertisement seeking quiet tenants after Darla's own sons left

for college. Darla hadn't wanted to house a teen-aged mother with a handicapped toddler. But she simply couldn't turn Marie away. Nor, it turned out, could she charge Marie and Paul rent.

Marie certainly struggled, but she finished college, obtained a teaching certificate and was hired to teach in the Hillsborough County schools. Three years ago she and Paul moved into the rented house they lived in now, and Darla was alone again.

Darla had saved Paul back then from a life of poverty and deprivation and the time she'd spent with him had taken its toll on them both. His irritability at the slightest frustration coupled with his total dependency and failure to develop normally became too much for her to handle. Now, Darla had grievously hurt him.

How could life be so cruel?

How could Marie ever forgive her?

Wouldn't it be better for Darla to rot in jail?

The volunteer handed Darla a visitor's pass, directing her to take the elevator to the third floor and then follow the blue line to the ICU waiting room.

Darla turned the corner and found Marie alone in the quiet room, her head leaned back against the wall, eyes closed. She wore jeans and a t-shirt, flip flops, no makeup. Her tear-streaked face stopped Darla cold.

Marie had been through hell already and there were more days of despair to follow.

Darla's own shame capsized her. Instead of concern for Marie and Paul, she'd worried only about herself. She'd run that little boy down with her car and then left him alone in the dark to suffer and die. What kind of woman had she become?

Marie shifted in the chair and opened her eyes.

"Oh, Darla!" she cried, rising to run toward her, holding onto

Darla as a drowning woman holds onto the last life raft, unaware that the raft is leaking.

Darla held Marie who cried until she was spent. Marie eventually stood apart, grasping her soggy tissues, and walked over to the small table for more.

"I thought I was through with tears. How much can one woman cry over a single child?" Marie asked seconds before her sobs began again.

Doctors long ago predicted Paul would never develop mental capacity beyond age five. He grew older and Marie watched class after class of her kindergarten students surpass Paul's ability. While he remained behind, Marie's heartache deepened. As he grew, becoming taller, heavier and harder to control, Marie often appeared at school with bruises where Paul had hit or kicked her.

Darla had suggested that Marie place Paul in a group home where he could get more specialized training and give Marie a much-needed break. Initially, she'd refused, denying the situation.

"I can handle Paul myself," she'd said.

Much later she'd placed Paul's name on the waiting list, but no place had opened for him in two years. If only Marie could have seen the obvious, Paul might not have been home last night at all. He wouldn't be lying here. Why hadn't Marie listened to Darla then?

Darla had consoled Marie through every crisis, offering the best guidance she could muster, sometimes hiring local lawyer Jennifer Lane to handle minor problems. But this was by far the most serious situation the three had faced. How would Marie get through this without Darla to rely upon?

"How is he?"

"Still unconscious. It looks like the car hit him in the side, knocked him down, and then ran over his legs and abdomen. He's had emergency surgery to repair broken bones and a lacerated liver caused by broken ribs. But they don't think he suffered a head injury, which may mean that he'll eventually be okay," Marie explained, all in one breath. Then, she grimaced, "Or at least as okay as Paul gets."

Darla heard Marie's desperate tone, but had already stopped listening to the words.

Paul would be all right; Darla hadn't killed him.

For the first time since the nightmares awakened her this morning, she began to think her life might not be over. They might get through this. She could, maybe, avoid jail. And if she did, she vowed she'd take care of Paul and Marie forever.

Marie drew ragged air into her lungs. "He was outside so long! He... they... If I ever find out who did this, who left him lying there like a dog! I swear, the bastard will rot in prison forever!"

CHAPTER FIVE

THE DOORBELL RANG JUST after seven o'clock. Darla looked through the peephole to see the uniformed officer waiting on the front porch. Kevin Cook. How long had he been there? Had he examined her car before coming to the door? Should she let him in?

The bell rang again. Darla steadied her nerves. Maybe if she was quiet, he'd think she wasn't home and go away. She placed both hands flat over her pounding heart. The bell rang insistently, followed by a sharp knock.

"Mrs. Nixon? Mrs. Nixon, are you home? Sheriff's office, Ma'am. Please open up."

She remembered his voice. She'd had confrontations with him when he was a child. Always rigid, belligerent, unwilling to compromise, he'd been a challenge then. Now, he was a threat.

Briefly, she considered ignoring him, calling Jennifer Lane to deal with him. But Kevin had always been single-minded, too. Focused to a fault. Like a leech on a warm-blooded animal, he never let go of anything voluntarily back then. A child's basic personality didn't change in adulthood, Darla knew. He'd hound her until he got what he needed.

"I'm coming!" she called, as if she'd just realized he was there.

Darla reached down, unlocked the door, and opened it wide.

"Why, it's Kevin Cook. How are you?" She held onto the door to keep her composure.

He ducked his head, acknowledging her greeting. "I'm fine, ma'am. It's good to see you again, after all these years. You look just the same."

Darla wasn't surprised by this statement. Her former students often said that.

"May I come in? I need to ask you a few questions about Paul Webster's accident."

She stood aside. He opened the door wider; maneuvered his broad body into the small room.

"I was back in the kitchen, making coffee. Would you like a cup?"

Perhaps he believed that explained her breathlessness, too. He'd removed his hat.

"No, ma'am. Thank you. I'm talking to everyone who attended the party at Ms. Webster's house last night. I have some questions to ask you and then I'll be on my way."

She smoothed the hem of her shirt over her slight hips and gestured. He sat on the davenport. She perched in the rocker opposite.

"How can I help?"

Detective Cook pulled a small spiral notebook and a pencil with a well-chewed eraser out of his shirt pocket. He flipped through the first few pages and folded the notebook open to a blank, ruled sheet. He jotted the date on the top and, after glancing at his watch, the time. He printed her name. Methodical and precise, as he'd been in elementary school.

"Ma'am, you left Ms. Webster's party around nine o'clock last night, is that right?"

The question was politely put, but Darla recognized the authority in his tone. She'd used the same tone herself in many a student disciplinary proceeding. Being the recipient was not pleasant.

"Yes."

"Did you see Paul Webster outside as you were leaving?"

He looked directly into her eyes as he asked the question. She wondered what he expected to see there, whether he imagined he had an innate ability to detect lies. Perhaps he did. She wouldn't lie, then. She didn't normally lie and she couldn't lie successfully, anyway.

Darla shook her head. Tears threatened. "I wish I had seen him, Kevin. I only wish I had."

Oh, how true that was. If she'd seen Paul, of course she wouldn't have hit him. None of this would have happened. Why hadn't she seen him?

She asked, "Why was he outside, anyway? I thought he was supposed to be staying the night with a neighbor?"

Officer Cook jerked his head back and forth, his mouth a thin line of disapproval. "The neighbor put him to bed around eight and didn't check on him again until morning. Apparently he left the house without her knowledge. We're guessing he wanted to go home. His mother said he didn't like being away from her overnight."

Darla's own concern about the neighborhood resurfaced. She knew the people who lived near Marie were generally unreliable. She'd asked Marie whether the woman could be trusted last night. Paul could be such a handful. Darla thought the woman might bring Paul home, unable to control him. But this level of negligence was too cruel.

Cook glanced at another page in his notebook again. "It was pretty dark out last night. Do you have trouble seeing in the dark?"

Surely, he knew the answer or he wouldn't have asked. He was trying to trick her into admitting what she'd done. She was guilty of reckless driving, at least. Her night vision was not sufficient to drive a car, and she'd driven anyway. And she'd hit a child, without even realizing it. She'd be treated with fewer leniencies than a drunk driver. Her judgment wasn't impaired. What could she say?

"It was raining. There aren't any streetlights on Marie's street. Maybe the county will get some up out there after this," Darla told him.

This wasn't a real answer and she was sure he realized it. A thin bead of sweat coated the area above her upper lip. She placed both hands flat on her thighs, fingers spread wide, holding steady.

Detective Cook was watching her closely. He printed notes on the clean spaces in his notebook, but she couldn't read his precise printing from this distance.

"You didn't see anyone hit Paul, then?"

"I didn't see Paul at all. I was concentrating on my driving."

Perspiration now appeared on her forehead. She wanted desperately to wipe it away. To prevent herself from doing so, she clasped her hands together and crossed her feet at the ankles.

"On a night like that, Paul shouldn't have been outside. Whoever hit him surely didn't mean to do it. But they should have stopped. Should have helped him right away," Detective

Cook said, as if he was talking to himself. He tapped the pencil led against the page. "Did you notice any other cars on the road as you left Ms. Webster's house?"

"No. I didn't. I think I was the first guest to leave, so the other cars were still in the driveway and parked along the street." Darla glanced at the coffee cup, but if she picked it up she'd spill coffee all over herself.

"Mrs. Nixon, the doctor says the biggest problem Paul has right now is how long he was left outside in the cold rain after he was hit. We're not sure exactly when that was, but it might have been about the time you were leaving." Kevin stopped a minute and flipped through the pages in his notebook, looking for something. "Are you sure you didn't see him?"

Darla couldn't answer again. She shook her head.

"Are you making any progress at all, Kevin? Finding whoever hit Paul?"

She'd tried not to ask, but the pressure to find out had overwhelmed her terror of his power to ruin her life.

Detective Cook watched her a bit longer before he said, "Hit and runs are hard to solve. If we don't get a break in the case in the next few days we may never solve it. That happens too often, I'm afraid."

"What kind of break are you hoping for?" Her voice sounded unnaturally high to her.

"Most often, the person driving the car just can't live with the guilt and turns himself in." Kevin's gaze was steady, pointed. He knew. Of course, he knew. Why would he be here otherwise? Why had she let him in? She should have called Jennifer Lane right away.

He added, "Or the boy could wake up and tell us who hit him."

A beat passed. Two. Darla began to tremble.

She'd been so happy that Paul was alive and would recover. She hadn't realized that if he woke up he might be able to identify her car as the one that hit him and fled the scene. He would send her to jail.

Her fist pounded absently on her thigh. Why did she drive that damn car after the doctor told her not to? Why?

Detective Cook closed the notebook. He returned it and the gnawed pencil to his pocket. When he stood, Darla rose with him. For just a moment, he seemed indecisive. Then his gaze fell on a picture frame on the table. She couldn't see the picture, but she knew it was there. She waited.

"Is that your younger son?" he asked, nodding in the direction of the picture.

"Yes. He graduated from Florida State last June," Darla said. "He's working in South America now."

"Those are amazing flowers in the background. What kind are they?"

Flowers? Were there flowers in the picture? She couldn't remember. She turned her upper body and her head far to the right to look. Too far. A person with normal peripheral vision would have been able to see the picture long before Darla could. Detective Cook observed her closely, his eyes narrowing just a bit.

"Oh, those are white birds of paradise. Lovely, aren't they?"

She turned back to face him, her nervousness apparent even to her. He should have known those blooms; they were common enough in Tampa. He was testing her.

Detective Cook remained quiet a bit too long.

"Yes," he said, nodding once for punctuation. "They are."

Then, he seemed to reach a decision, turned and walked to

the door. Darla followed a few feet behind. He opened the screen and stepped outside, placed his hat on his head, and turned to face her through the mesh.

"I hope you don't mind, but I examined your car before I came up to the door. It's got quite a few dents in it."

Darla nodded. "It's embarrassing, really."

"Have you reported all those incidents to your insurance company, Ma'am?"

The insurance company kept all reports. He'd be able to subpoena them if he hadn't already. Jennifer Lane couldn't prevent the disclosure, even if Darla called her now and confessed everything.

Darla's mouth was dry. She wet her lips with her tongue.

"I can't afford to pay any more insurance than I'm already paying."

"I see," he said. "Well, thank you for your help, Mrs. Nixon. You sure scared the heck out of me when I was a boy," he said with a grin before he turned to leave. "But you're just a regular person, aren't you? Not scary at all. You take care, now."

She watched him walk down the sidewalk, enter his patrol car, back completely out of the driveway, and head toward town. Only then did she close the door. Only then did she sob.

CHAPTER SIX

MARIE HADN'T LEFT THE hospital since she'd found Paul lying broken, near death on the side of the road a week earlier. She slept no more than fifty-five minutes of any hour in the waiting room's plastic seats each night. She approached Paul's bedside to hold his hand and whisper to him for the five minutes of every hour she was allowed around the clock. The hospital staff had surrendered their efforts to persuade her to go home and rest. Guilt attached her to her child's bedside, Darla knew.

Guilt also appended Darla to Marie's suffering every evening after work. Darla arranged a paid leave of absence for Marie. A substitute teacher handled Marie's classes. Under the circumstances, this was the least Darla could do. Marie had no savings and wouldn't be able to pay her bills or for Paul's medical care if she lost her job.

Each evening a taxi brought Darla to share Marie's vigil. She bore Marie's clean clothes and food for dinner. Marie prayed for Paul constantly. Darla prayed for him, too, knowing full well that when he awakened she would then be asked to exchange her life for his. It was a sacrifice she would willingly make, but she was reminded of the admonition to be wary of answered prayers. When Paul woke up, then Darla would call Jennifer Lane; she'd need a good lawyer.

"Kevin Cook was here today," Marie said as she pretended to chew on the Cuban sandwich Darla had delivered. She sipped a bit of hot coffee and tried to wash the lump of bread and meat past her gullet. Marie had lost at least ten pounds in the past week, weight she couldn't spare.

Marie said, "It was so hard. Kevin asked me about Paul's life and I didn't know what to say."

The bones in her face were as prominent as an emaciated corpse. Her shiny blonde hair now fell in dirty strands about her shoulders. Gone was the happy, celebratory young woman of a few nights ago.

Darla understood exactly what Marie meant. Paul was not an easy child. Sweet and loving one minute, angry and abusive the next; he still wet the bed at night. Many times, Marie had been reduced to tears of helplessness and frustration. Darla had tried to suggest alternatives for Paul, but Marie had ignored them.

Yet, Marie loved her son, as most mothers love their children, regardless of bad behavior. Darla had seen such misplaced love many, many times in parent conferences. Parental ambivalence was normal.

"Any progress on the investigation?" Darla asked, changing the focus, hoping the answer would be no.

Marie moved her head back and forth. "He says they've done all they can. They're sending the file up to the Florida Department of Law Enforcement. But he says it doesn't look good for finding out who did it."

A few tears dripped from Marie's eyes and she ignored

them. Darla wondered where the water came from. Marie had cried so much in the past week that she should have been totally dehydrated by now.

"If Paul… doesn't wake up…" Marie began and the tears intensified. She took a sip of the coffee as Darla put her arm around Marie's shoulders for comfort. She felt the bony shoulders and skinny arms underneath Marie's cotton shirt. "… then it will be a vehicular homicide. But that won't make the case easier to solve."

Darla gave her another squeeze. "Oh, honey. No matter who hit Paul, it's done. We can't rewind the clock and make this go away. We have to face reality." *Like I wish I'd done,* Darla thought. She tried to soothe Marie's hurt, but the words seemed to enrage her.

"The bastard owes us an apology, Darla! He needs to lie in a hospital bed with his body all banged up. He needs to suffer!" Marie broke down completely then, sobs overtaking her as they had so many times in the past week.

Darla removed the coffee cup from her hand and took the sandwich away. She buried Marie's head in her own shoulder and patted her while her ragged sobs continued.

"I'm sorry, Marie, honey. I'm so, so sorry this has happened."

But Darla's apology didn't soothe Marie at all. "Oh, Darla. We'd had a big fight, Paul and me. It's my fault. He didn't want to go. I shouldn't have made him stay overnight away from home. I should have kept him with me. You know how upset he gets if he's away from me too long. I shouldn't have left him there."

"Shush, honey. It's not your fault. You thought he was safe." Darla continued to hold her, trying to make her feel better in this impossible situation, wondering how much longer Darla would be around to take care of them both.

"But the very last thing I said to him was so mean! I told him I needed time to myself, without him!" Marie broke down then, sobbing and inconsolable. "What have I done?"

CHAPTER SEVEN

WHEN DARLA ENTERED THE waiting room three nights later, the atmosphere felt different. Yesterday, Marie had seemed to be recovering from the shock of Paul's injuries and resigned to waiting for his recovery. Now, Marie's face bore the evidence of fresh tears.

"What's happened, honey?" Darla asked her, setting down the brown paper bag in which she'd packed their banana sandwiches and milk.

The question brought new pain. Marie turned her stricken face toward Darla and gasped for air. "Paul had a seizure last night," she said, her voice a low whisper.

Darla looked over into the ICU bed. At first, Paul seemed the same. He lay motionless, casts on both legs, his right arm in traction, and countless tubes running into and from his small body. Yet, the freckles that splashed his entire face seemed darker, the visible skin between them more pale. His hair was pasted to his skull. And then she saw that he was now hooked up to life support. She could hear the rhythm of the ventilator. For some reason, Paul couldn't breathe.

"What did Dr. Baker say?"

Marie hiccoughed and wiped her nose with the back of her hand. Her voice was so low that Darla had to lean in closer to hear.

"He said Paul will never wake up." Marie's eyes were full of remorse. "He wants to discontinue life support. So many times, I thought how much easier my life would be without Paul. And now," Marie's voice caught again, "now I can't believe I'm going to lose him."

Eventually, she sobbed herself into an exhausted sleep and Darla could only hold her.

Around midnight, Dr. Baker returned with his consent forms. Life support was discontinued a few hours later and Paul died peacefully, his mother by his side and Darla holding his hand.

Both women cried until they could cry no more, but Darla realized that at least some of their tears were caused by relief.

CHAPTER EIGHT

THE DAY AFTER PAUL'S funeral, Darla sat across the desk from Jimmy Finch, another of her former students. She couldn't bring herself to call Jennifer Lane after all. Jennifer was Marie's lawyer. Wouldn't Jennifer be ethically bound to tell Marie? Nor could she call Willa Carson, no matter what. Not now. Now, Darla was guilty of murder.

Finch listened without revealing his thoughts or feelings. Did he think her actions cruel or merely reckless? He was the only lawyer she knew well enough to approach who didn't travel in her social circle. She'd never needed a lawyer for herself before. After her divorce, which had been deceptively simple, her ex-husband fled the state and she'd had no further contact with him. Her parents died without enough assets to create a problem bigger than her tax accountant could resolve. Her sons had never been in trouble. No, a lawyer had never been required. Until now.

"How long have you known you have RP?" Jimmy asked her, making notes on the yellow legal pad with a cheap ballpoint. The action reminded her of Kevin Cook. She shuddered.

"About twenty years, I guess. It was diagnosed in my early thirties." Darla never talked about her RP; verbalizing refreshed the fright she'd felt when the doctors had first explained her condition.

He reviewed the notes he'd written and summarized. "You had your last eye exam more than a month before this incident. Your doctor told you to stop driving, especially at night. You disregarded that advice. And you drove at a time when your impaired night vision affected your ability to see clearly and you hit a child with your car." He stopped and looked up at her a moment. "Have I got that right?"

Darla nodded miserably, shocked to hear how harsh the words sounded.

"Were you drinking at the party?"

"Coffee. I don't drink and drive," her tone a bit more judgmental than a woman in her situation should have been.

He wrote that down, too, then reviewed his notes.

"Why didn't you stop the car that night?"

"If I'd thought for one second that I'd hit anyone, I would have stopped. I know it's a crime to leave the scene of an accident. But, I thought I hit a trash bag. It was so dark out and raining and, well, I just…" her voice trailed off.

Jimmy Finch leaned forward and folded his hands over the top of the legal pad. He studied her for a bit. She wished she could read his mind, to know what he was thinking. He began a series of bewildering questions and statements that confused Darla further.

"How do you know a plastic trash bin *didn't* hit your car and you *didn't* run over a trash bag?"

Bewildered by his change of attitude, she could only stare. What was he saying?

"You left the party. It was dark, raining, windy. Garbage bags and cans lined the road. Something hit your car. You thought it was a plastic trashcan, blown by the wind. Then, you rolled over what you thought was a plastic trash bag that had spilled from the can. You didn't stop to check, right?" he sounded so reasonable now. "So, again, why do you think, now, that you might have hit a child?"

The question shocked her. Since she'd heard about Paul's accident, she'd believed, absolutely, that she'd been the one to hit him. But Finch was right. She didn't *know*. Not *for sure*. There were a number of other people at Marie's that night. More traffic on the street than usual. And she didn't know exactly when Paul had been hit.

Maybe it wasn't her fault. Maybe she didn't do it.

Her heart began to pound so rapidly she couldn't breathe. She tried to rise from her chair and her legs wouldn't hold her weight. But she'd never know for sure. The uncertainty couldn't be resolved.

After a few seconds, Finch took a deep breath and let it out slowly. He set the legal pad down, folded his hands over his protruding stomach, and watched her.

"We need to think about the car."

"I haven't driven since that night," she began.

He held up a hand, palm out, firm. "No. Don't tell me anything yet. Hear me out."

He didn't say, "Too bad you didn't stop driving when the doctor told you to." But Darla heard those words just the same.

"Mrs. Nixon, I'm your lawyer. And what you've told me is confidential. But if you think you hit a child, if your car was involved in a vehicular homicide, there will be trace evidence. Every part of an automobile can be identified. The best thing to do is to turn the car over to the police. If you give them the car, they'll be able to match whatever forensic trace evidence they have to your exact vehicle. And, as it's your car, and you live alone with no other drivers in your household... Well, it's very likely the police will conclude that you were the driver who hit Paul. I'm sorry."

Jimmy Finch had always been sorry. He was a sorry student and a sorry human being. Darla remembered this, too late.

He seemed to read her thoughts, for he added, "Any other lawyer would give you the same advice."

After a few moments, he continued. "But, if you don't believe you hit a child with your car, then I have no ethical obligation to contact the police and I wouldn't advise you to do so, either. It all depends on what you tell me."

"What should I do, then?" she wondered aloud.

"If you did hit the child, even if the reason you hit him was that you couldn't see due to your RP, the act was perhaps reckless driving, but nothing more. You might not have been charged with anything that night. The serious crime you may have committed was leaving the scene of the accident and failing to come forward once you knew that the child had been hit. There are no witnesses to the crime and if you don't confess, it's unlikely you'd be convicted." He stopped for emphasis. "The evidence against you just doesn't exist. In this case, silence is golden."

Perhaps in response to the horrified look on her face, he softened his tone a bit.

He said, "No one knows that your doctor told you to stop driving. Marie Webster will testify that she saw you behind the wheel of the car that evening, but she didn't see you hit Paul. Nor did anyone else. The time of the incident isn't fixed very well because Marie didn't find Paul until the next morning. He could have been hit at any time during the night."

Jimmy Finch pushed back in his chair and folded one leg over the other. "It's likely you'll get away with this. Now that Paul's dead, what good will it do for you to confess?" He threw her a lifeline then. "Or maybe it wasn't your car at all. Maybe someone else hit Paul, not you. Have you ever considered that?"

Darla had replayed the incident a thousand times in her mind. She saw the darkness, felt the thud against the side of her car and the rough ride as she ran over Paul's body after she hit him.

No, she'd done it. There was no doubt in her mind. She was guilty.

"Let me just say one more thing, Mrs. Nixon," the pious Jimmy Finch intoned. "The time for you to have fixed this situation is long past. You shouldn't have been driving that night at all. And you should have come forward the next morning when you first found out about Paul's injury and realized you might have hit him. This deceitful behavior is not like you, Mrs. Nixon. Not at all."

She hated him then, for a moment, all the more because what he said was true and no less than she'd told herself time and time again.

Finch leaned forward, earnestly. "But think very carefully about what you do now. Everyone makes mistakes. As adults, we must all live with our transgressions. That guilty knowledge feels like a curse and changes your life forever. If you tell someone, once you share the harm, there is the chance that you will feel better. But the person you tell will suffer, too. Perhaps more than you have. Even if that person forgives you."

"I can't just let this go," Darla almost wailed in despair,

realizing that was exactly what her lawyer was advising her to do.

"No? What will Marie do if you go to prison? Does she have anyone else to turn to? The fact is that confession doesn't erase what's already happened. You can't bring Paul back to life no matter what you try. Never forget that."

He needn't worry. She wouldn't confess. She'd apologized to Marie a thousand times, but no apology would soothe Marie's soul. Marie's own guilt at wishing herself childless and failing to check on her son that night consumed her as much as the hatred she bore for her son's killer. For in Marie's mind, Paul's accident was nothing less than cold-blooded murder.

Never mind that Dr. Baker had assured Marie the delay in Paul's treatment hadn't affected the outcome. The seizure was unexpected, a bad break, and it probably would have occurred if Paul had been rushed to the hospital immediately. Indeed, as the seizure was unexplained, it could have happened in the absence of any trauma at all. Paul might have died at home, in his own bed, any time. Medical science simply couldn't say.

Darla knew she was rationalizing her decision even as she did so.

But Jimmy Finch was right; knowing Darla's fault would not console Marie. Nor would it help Marie to have her only friend jerked away now when she needed a friend more than anything.

No, Darla would not confess. Her punishment was to live with her guilt and regret. She already felt the heavy weight of a punishment worse than anything the justice system could do to her if she was ever caught.

But she would never drive again.

CHAPTER NINE

THREE YEARS LATER, DARLA was legally blind. Severe tunnel vision prevented her from doing her job. In the gathering darkness of her RP, Darla could no longer read or watch television. She lived in a closed environment of her own making.

She often examined the secret she longed to share to absolve herself of crushing guilt. But the devastating impact her confession would have on Marie wasn't worth relieving Darla's burning desire to tell her secret. Nor would confession relieve her heartache.

How could she ever feel better knowing that she'd killed a child? No. Her punishment was keeping that guilt to herself. She felt the constant pain as no less than she deserved.

"All you can do is move on. Help Marie. And be a good person," she told herself. She'd been a principal, one who'd always set a good example for her students. No more.

She would never forget, yet she craved forgiveness. That's all she wanted. For Marie to forgive her. To forgive herself. But Darla expected to go to her own grave unforgiven, even as Marie returned to the vivacious teacher she'd been before.

Marie had hosted a retirement party last year at Darla's home, an abode they once again shared. Jennifer Lane attended, but Darla did not confess to her, either.

The bittersweet absence of Paul was like constant sucking on a sore tooth. The mug Paul had given Darla that last Christmas had been pushed to the very back of an unused cupboard. Darla could still see it whenever she closed her eyes and felt the gap in her heart where Paul used to be.

The mug, and Marie's vivid presence, punished Darla daily for her one act of criminal behavior in a life filled with service to her community. Even if the law said otherwise, Darla felt like a killer.

Each year, Detective Kevin Cook had visited on the eve of the anniversary of Paul's accident, to admit he'd made no progress in the investigation.

On the third visit, Detective Cook sat on the davenport as he had that first evening so long ago. He seemed reluctant to speak, uncomfortable in his skin. "I wanted to let you know that the statute of limitations on the vehicular homicide case, assuming we could ever have proved it, expires today. We might be able to charge the driver with concealment later, but that's not likely."

Darla knew what this meant. Paul's killer would never be punished now, no matter what. The knowledge didn't comfort her.

He sat in Darla's living room, with his little notebook on his knee, another chewed pencil poised above the pages, pleading.

Cook asked, "Have you heard *anything* new that might help us? It's our last chance."

So he knew, Darla realized. Now that she couldn't see him, she could feel his despair. He'd known all along. He knew it was her. She should just tell him and get it over with. What did she have to lose now, anyway? She lived in a dark world that imprisoned her more effectively than any cell to which she might once have been sentenced.

Darla had imagined this moment so many times. She'd rehearsed her confession, watched Detective Cook arrest her. She imagined he would enjoy that, after all the punishments she'd meted out to him when she was his principal. She opened her mouth to say the words, but she could not force herself to speak.

An older and wiser Marie took her hand. "Thank you for coming by, Kevin. We don't know anything more about Paul's death. And, to be honest, it opens old wounds for you to come here every year. If you find the driver of the car, then please let us know. But otherwise, we should close this chapter in our lives and try to move on."

Detective Kevin Cook's expression barely changed at first. But then, Darla could feel the force of his anger overwhelm him. *No,* she wanted to shout, petrified now of being accused, of losing Marie, too. *Leave us alone.*

He stood up, replaced his hat, removed his handcuffs from his belt and opened them. Darla heard the clicking and braced herself for the steel's cold bracelets restraining her wrists.

He said, officially, "Marie Webster, you are under arrest for second degree murder, reckless disregard of human life, in connection with the death of your son, Paul Webster."

What was he saying? What was he doing?

He reached down and grabbed Marie's forearm. Darla heard him click the cuffs on one wrist and then the other. She didn't protest.

"You have the right to remain silent, anything you do say can and will be used against you... "

Darla cried out. "Marie? You didn't kill Paul! I know you didn't!"

No, this wasn't possible. She knew Marie. Paul's mother would never, ever have hurt him. When the roaring in her head subsided, she heard Marie's soft crying.

Cook finished reciting her rights.

Marie turned to Darla and placed her wet cheek next to Darla's own. Their tears mingled. "I'm so sorry. I wanted to be the mother you were, the woman you always thought I was. But I just couldn't deal with it all anymore. Paul was too much. I couldn't handle him alone."

What was she saying? Darla had practically raised Marie and Paul both. Her Marie wouldn't have, couldn't have, been so calculating.

"But you were home that night." Darla said, bewildered, uncomprehending. She'd lived with crushing guilt for three long years. How could she have been so wrong about everything?

Marie's tone was subdued. "I went out after everyone left, to pick up another bottle of vodka. I was so happy and I just wanted the celebration to last a little longer. It was on the way back... I didn't realize I'd hit him until it was too late. He just ran out in front of the car and I—I couldn't stop. I got out and he was lying there and I knew that if I didn't help him, he would die." She whispered the last, so quietly Darla leaned forward to hear. "He would die, and I'd be free."

Darla shook her head as if to clear it of years of debris that blocked her insight. She couldn't accept Marie's confession, couldn't believe it.

"But, Paul died of a seizure. You didn't kill him."

Marie said nothing more. She didn't have to.

Slowly, Darla realized that Marie must have done something

to Paul in the hospital, too. Something to finish the job she'd started on the night she'd been named *Teacher of the Year.*

"Do you have someone you can call to help you, Mrs. Nixon?" Detective Kevin Cook asked her kindly as he escorted Marie out the front door.

Darla, bereft, tears streaming down her face, nodded. "Yes," she whispered.

As she dialed Marie's lawyer, Darla's heart felt a glimmer of hope it hadn't held for three long years.

THE END

FATAL
ENEMY

For Robert

CHAPTER ONE

JESS KIMBALL SWITCHED THE Glock's grip to her left hand, raised her right to rub her sore neck and stretched her shoulders. Her body seemed to hum at the cellular level. She felt fatigued, yet buzzingly alert. She hadn't been in the same room with Richard Martin for more than a dozen years. Worse things than Richard had happened to her since she'd seen him last. He'd find out soon enough that she wasn't a gullible sixteen-year-old anymore.

Dressed crown to sole in black, sitting as still as the furniture, Jess was indistinguishable from her surroundings. Ambient light was non-existent in the quiet neighborhood, where *crime* should've been non-existent. The microwave clock glowed 3:00:15 a.m. providing the room's only illumination.

Jess leaned back, ankles crossed, heels propped on the kitchen table, and settled in to wait through the remainder of the third night. A bouquet of Stargazer lilies stood across the room but their fragrant perfume filled the air like oxygen. Richard was allergic to Stargazers. Jess appreciated the subtle torture although she hadn't planned it.

Man, she hated custody battles; the children always lose. But this custody dispute was different, more vital. She couldn't refuse to help this time because the victim was Richard Martin's daughter. Knowing Richard as she did would make the difference between success and failure.

As malevolent a bastard as ever drew breath, Richard was far from stupid. He would try to steal Anna until someone stopped him. If not tonight, then tomorrow or another night soon. Jess felt it, yes. Instinct and preparation had saved her life before. She wouldn't ignore them now. But hunches were not enough.

Her throat was parched, but she couldn't risk a trip to the faucet for water. Time seemed stagnant even as the clock reflected 3:10:21 a.m. Combating boredom, her thoughts wandered again to Richard when she'd been in lust with him. Inside the ski mask, her face burned now with a different heat. He'd been her first romance when she was sixteen and seeking love wherever she could find it. She'd felt as treasured as a rare art object for about three weeks. The warning signs were there if only she'd been sophisticated enough to recognize them. She wasn't. She'd made a significant mistake a long time ago, and it had defined her life evermore.

Undisclosed petty crimes and scandals had blown the Martin family into her town, and serious crimes hastened them away a year later. Richard had turned eighteen as his crimes escalated. He'd have gone to prison. A chill ran through her as she recalled how narrowly she'd escaped his bondage when Richard's parents rushed him to a new jurisdiction moments before his arrest for grand theft auto.

Jess stretched again, shifted the gun purposefully at 3:12:46 a.m. She noted its heft increasing with the slightest attention paid during the passing seconds. *Show yourself, Richard, you coward.*

Richard never knew that he'd left her pregnant with Peter. Nor had he cared. Jess's embarrassed adolescent pride kept the news from him at first. Later, when she realized his miserable domination for what it was, she concealed Peter from Richard and vowed she always would. Not that he'd ever looked back. Jess was grateful for that much.

She'd never told anyone who'd fathered her son. Nor would she. When people asked, she simply said she didn't know. If pressed for more details, she said she'd been raped by an unknown assailant who was never apprehended, which was technically accurate but not true. She'd been a minor back then and Richard was not, so what he'd done was statutory rape and he'd have gone to jail if anyone had bothered to report his crime. But she'd been a willing participant in his seduction. Still, "rape" described precisely how she felt when Richard tossed her aside like a used rag. Maybe that was when anger's spark lodged firmly in her gut and flamed whenever Richard's name was mentioned.

So far, the rape answer had sufficed. No one ever tried to hunt down a man Jess Kimball couldn't find for herself. People assumed an investigative journalist of her stature, coupled with her national crusade for victims' rights, made Jess infallible as a prison-trained bloodhound. Which was true.

3:23:07 a.m. How much longer should she wait tonight? At least until dawn. She'd promised Betsy. And then she'd be back tomorrow. Richard had told Betsy he was coming, simply to terrorize her further. Jess would be waiting for as long as it took.

Jess inhaled deeply, drawing the Stargazers' fragrance into her lungs and remembered how she'd watched Richard's life from afar. Memories heated her temper and chased away the last of the early morning chill. He'd cut a wide swathe through a long list of gullible girls and later, gullible women. None of them were foolish enough to deliver his child afterward, but each one bore invisible scars Jess could easily discern just the same.

Until seven years ago when Richard seized sexier, younger, naive, sensitive and fragile Betsy. She never stood a chance.

Jess had contacted Betsy back then, tried to warn her before she married him, but Betsy's inexperience prevailed. Thus began the destructive tango that led them all here.

All these years later, Jess felt grateful to have escaped Richard's cruelty but guilty, too. *Survivor guilt* was what the psychologists called it. Irrational perhaps, but real enough. She shrugged; she supposed Richard had to marry someone eventually. He wasn't a man who'd remain single forever and Jess couldn't save all the Betsys in the world. She prayed silently, *Just this one, please.*

Jess wagged her head back and forth and stretched her neck, attempting to push the fatigue and the memories away. But her stress had long ago settled into knots harder than obsidian. She needed to stand, walk out the tension, but she couldn't risk being discovered. Failure was not an option. Not this time. She tried to focus on something other than her screaming muscles.

She couldn't keep her gaze from the microwave clock. *Only 3:34:17 a.m. Would this night never end?*

Betsy had never asked why Jess agreed to help her and thus spared the lies. Betsy didn't know Richard had fathered a son or that Peter was kidnapped. Betsy presented Jess with a second chance to save Betsy and her daughter before Richard destroyed them as he'd destroyed Jess and Peter. Maybe Betsy had forgotten her worth, but Jess would not. Nor would she allow Richard to harm Peter's half-sister. Someday his sister's DNA would help Jess prove Peter's identity.

When she found Peter, he'd have both his sister *and* his mother.

Jess avoided the ultimate question her son was sure to ask one day: "Why did you put my father in prison?"

At 3:54:17 a.m., as if her thoughts had conjured him, she heard Richard's heavy tread on the squeaky plank decking. Every nerve stood at attention while she remained as still as the lilies.

Jess pressed the remote button to activate the security camera outside the back door. The night vision would record every moment in an eerie green glow. She'd have the one thing she needed to nail the bastard—evidence.

She blended with the darkness and waited, holding the Glock in her right hand, ready to use it. But not too soon. Jess knew the law inside out. Only when Richard left the premises with Anna would he be guilty of kidnapping. Only then. Not a moment before.

Should she be forced to confront him earlier, he'd claim he wasn't taking Anna anywhere. A court would agree. Betsy was the custodial parent, but Richard had bought and still owned this house. Technically, he wasn't trespassing and he could visit whenever he chose. His twisted lies and intimidation had persuaded Betsy to excuse his behavior repeatedly.

Not this time. Jess would have irrefutable evidence and she'd use it effectively, just as she had when he stole that Jaguar all those years ago.

So Jess had to allow Richard to accomplish the crimes he'd come to commit instead of interrupting him in the act as Betsy had done twice before. Kidnapping would send him away for life, if there was any justice at all in the world.

But a just world would have locked Richard Martin up long

ago before he raped Jess. A just world would never have taken Peter. The only just world Jess believed in was the one she created herself.

Watching the microwave clock, she timed him. Richard spent exactly twelve seconds forcing the lock and opening the back door. She smiled again. He should have tried his old key. She'd made sure it would work, just in case he proved less predictable than she'd expected. Overconfidence kills, that much she knew. But she knew him better than anyone else. Maybe better than he knew himself.

The security alarm began its incessant bleat the moment Richard opened the door. Jess breathed silently, disturbing the air as little as possible. He had the instincts of an apex predator at the top of the food chain and the top of his game. He would sense her presence if she made the slightest sound.

He crossed the tile to the alarm panel next to the refrigerator. He rapid-punched the six numbers of his wedding date, the code he and Betsy had chosen when he still lived here. Before their bitter divorce.

The alarm stopped well within the window of acceptable Miami PD response time.

He turned toward the next goal of his mission, never glancing in her direction. So predictable.

Arrogance was always Richard's Achilles' heel. It simply didn't occur to him that anyone would be watching. Jess grinned again inside the black ski mask she wore over her head and face.

Richard climbed the stairs and covered the short distance to the first door on the right while Jess watched from the shadows. He paused. The nightlights she'd placed illuminated him enough that the camera would record perfectly.

As if he followed Jess's script, Richard wore no head

covering. He showed his face to avoid frightening his daughter if she awakened, to keep her quiet and not arouse her mother in the room down the hallway. Betsy's sheer terror tomorrow morning when she found Anna missing was much of what the sadist wanted to accomplish. He wanted Betsy off balance and afraid. Which she was almost all the time.

Every move Richard made reinforced Jess's sense of justification. She hadn't been near him since she was a child herself but she was satisfied that he really was the bastard she believed him to be. Reassured, she felt free to follow through without remorse.

Richard glanced around, maybe confirming that Betsy still slept soundly, that Miami PD hadn't received the silent alarm. After a moment, he opened the door to Anna's room and crept inside.

He emerged shortly with the sleeping girl in his arms. Anna was dressed in white pajamas. Strawberry curls framed her cherubic face and cascaded down the back of his arm. Partly because she always slept soundly, and partly because Jess had given her a mild sedative before bed, the child didn't stir. She hated leaving the girl in Richard's arms even a moment. Jess hoped Anna would never know anything about this evening and would sleep straight through.

Richard eased the door almost closed, leaving it as Betsy had when she saw her daughter last so that she wouldn't know Anna was gone until she saw the empty bed. *Bastard.* He descended the stairs in silence but for a stifled sneeze.

Jess waited. Her right hand held the Glock firmly pointed in Richard's direction. She'd shoot him only if he forced her to. But shoot him, she would. He'd be a fool to believe otherwise.

She *knew* Richard. If he saw her before she was ready, he

would do something stupid. Something that might hurt Anna. The child's safety was paramount. Jess steadied herself and remained invisible as long as possible.

Richard snuck out the back door and closed it without a sound. Only then did she move.

Jess activated the tiny camera she wore in a pendant around her neck, waited until she heard the creaking boards under his feet and three sneezes in a row before she hurried silently out behind him. A cool breeze brushed across her eyes and lips, the only uncovered parts of her body.

She followed Richard off the property and onto the street where he'd parked a dark SUV. A less arrogant man might have noticed he was being followed. Richard did not. Now. Now he'd taken Anna in the eyes of the law. Jess wasted no time gloating.

He was bent over, placing Anna in the back seat when Jess came up behind him and pressed the Glock briefly to his spine before she widened the distance between them beyond his arm's reach.

"Move away from the car. Much as I'd like to shoot you..." She allowed her husky voice to trail away. Disuse and fear had stolen the moisture from her mouth, but she refused to acknowledge it. She moved her tongue imperceptibly seeking saliva.

Richard stepped back, cavalierly raised both hands palms out, as if he was play-acting with a child.

"Turn around," she said, quietly, hoping not to awaken Anna. He complied. He saw the gun, pointed now at his chest. He smirked.

"Smile," she said, picking up the pendant and pointing the micro camera directly toward him. "A picture's worth a year of testimony, isn't it?"

She snapped three photographs of Anna sleeping in the vehicle, too. Each image would be date and time stamped. Evidence. The more, the better.

She'd argued with Betsy and her sister, Bette, for hours about the next part of their plan. Betsy had cried, said she didn't want her child's father incarcerated. She wasn't desperate enough yet.

But Jess knew Betsy would be more desperate later; it was a mistake not to finish this now, once and for all. Richard would never give up as long as he drew free breath. Letting him go was a stupid mistake. Yet this was not her decision to make.

The breeze had picked up force and dried her eyeballs each time it brushed across, yet she refused to blink. Too much could happen in the blink of an eye. Peter was stolen in what seemed just such a quick moment fifteen years ago.

Jess held the gun steady and waited for Richard to make his move. Maybe he would give her the excuse she needed to do what should be done. Could she shoot him if she had to? *In a New York second.*

Released and alone, Richard would steal his daughter again, not because he loved her, but because he *owned* her. Anna would never be safe from him. Ever. He should have gone to prison long ago for battering his wife. Or when he stole Anna the last two times. But Betsy had refused to testify against him. Now, Jess had proof when Betsy needed it. But it would have been so much better if Betsy had agreed to Jess's final solution. Jess knew Richard was a fatal enemy, not a mere opponent.

Richard stared at Jess, wary but unafraid. He seemed to know her, but not recognize her simultaneously. His puzzlement was almost comical.

Jess's slender frame was indistinguishable from a slight

man's in these clothes. And she held an equalizer pointed at his heart. Did he recognize her voice? Maybe, although they hadn't talked in years and he'd been through a lot of women since then.

She could almost see him calculating his next move and five moves after that, like a chess match. Richard had always been good at strategic games.

Jess said what she'd agreed to say. "If you ever set foot in the state of Florida again, the video of tonight's escapade will be delivered to the U.S. Attorney's office. You'll die in prison."

He smirked again. He wasn't afraid of her. He was a fool.

Jess's hand itched to smash the gun into his face at least, but she kept calm. The video would be her shield, not his sword against her, no matter how much she'd rather finish this now.

"Move to the front of the car," she said.

He sidled to the center in front of the grille, well lit by the streetlight and far enough away. Her gaze never leaving him, the gun steady, Jess bent down and lifted the little girl. Anna stirred, but didn't waken. Jess almost cried when she smelled Anna's fabric softener and baby shampoo scents.

Bastard.

When she was sure Anna was secure in her grasp, Jess distanced herself from Richard's SUV.

"Get in and drive away," she instructed, her tone harder this time, annealed with years of hatred.

Hands in his pockets, Richard shrugged, sauntered around to the driver's side and opened the front door. Instantly, the car alarm sounded. Impossibly loud repeated long blasts of the horn invaded the suburban nighttime, blasting Jess's ears.

The cacophony awakened Anna. When she saw the black-clad apparition holding her, she began to cry and kick, yelling "Let me go! Let me go!"

Jess struggled, grabbed her tightly to keep her from taking them both down to the ground, but the gun's steady aim didn't waver.

"Hush, Anna," Jess whispered close to her ear. "It's Aunt Jess. It's okay. Be quiet now."

"Aunt Jess?" the astonished child cried, tears and screams coming to a shaky, tentative halt. She pulled the ski-mask off Jess's head in one quick grab exposing her hot face to the cool morning breeze.

Richard now had one leg into the SUV, his weight shifted toward the driver's seat. He pressed the key fob to silence the blasting horn, and then flashed his sardonic smirk again. "Nice to see you again, Jess. You didn't grow up much, did you?"

She stiffened and extended the gun, her intention clear. "Don't forget what I told you, Richard. No contact. Go."

He moved his head slowly, side to side, smirk firmly affixed. "Think again, little girl. I'm taking orders from you?" He laughed, slid into the SUV, started the engine, rolled down the window, and aimed a stare of pure hatred her way.

Jess shivered imperceptibly. She'd made an open enemy of a distant one. Somehow, he would prove he controlled her, too, along with everything else in his world, no matter what the cost.

She felt hot fear coursing through her entire body and a quick flash of insight. Could he be the one who'd stolen Peter? She'd investigated and rejected the possibility long ago because Richard didn't know Peter existed. Had she been wrong?

She couldn't speak. She held the gun steady, pointed at his head.

All pretext of the gentleness he'd shown his daughter gone, he said, "You'll be sorry you screwed me, Jess. Count on it."

The SUV's powerful engine roared louder than a six-pack of

Blue Angles as he sped away in the quiet darkness of the early suburban morning.

She watched his taillights recede to red pinpoints and disappear around a corner before she whispered aloud.

"I've been sorry about that for years and years."

CHAPTER TWO

THE NEWS FROM THE amber alert Internet subscription service flashed across her computer as she worked on revisions to her most recent investigative article for *Taboo Magazine*. She ignored the alert several times until she reached a logical stopping point. A domestic violence call in a Miami neighborhood. Every nerve in her body vibrated the instant Jess read the address. Eyebrows gathered at the bridge of her nose reflecting her pain when she squeezed her eyes shut and covered her face with both hands in the only brief moment of regret she allowed herself now. More pain would follow, as it should.

Her fingers shook as she worked the keys for information, hoping she was wrong while certain she wasn't.

The first officer at the scene found a woman shot and a five-year-old girl missing. An amber alert went out at 4:15 a.m. Jess glanced down at the clock on the screen. Twenty-five minutes ago. Wasting no time on useless recriminations, she left immediately.

Thirty minutes later, she reached Saturn Circle, a few houses scattered around the cul-de-sac bordering Lake Tarpon. Miami

PD cruisers blocked the Dolphin Avenue entrance. Jess parked the rental and slipped her Glock under the front seat. She had a license to carry, but no need to make this tense situation worse.

She grabbed her laptop and approached the first officer she saw.

"Hey, Randy," she said, as powerfully as she could muster simply to avoid startling him in the darkness. She showed her ID. She'd been working in Miami for several weeks on another story. The cops she'd met were helpful and sympathetic. No one wanted to help crime victims within the bounds of the law more than Jess did, and she always made sure local law enforcement knew that. They were all on the same team, she felt.

Officer Randy Wilson wagged his head, rubbed his neck. "Sorry. No media inside. What's your interest, anyway?"

Jess met his steady gaze. "Betsy Martin is a crime victim. I came to offer support."

"She doesn't need it," Randy told her, too bluntly.

Jess released her breath in a long exhale, closed her eyes. The news hit her hard in the gut, even though she'd expected it, really. Pressing a man like Richard as hard as she'd done was dangerous. She'd known it at the time, but she'd thought the stakes were worth it. A short moment of guilty mourning was all she permitted herself for now. Plenty of time for remorse later, too.

"Suspects?"

"Nasty divorce. Custody problems with the daughter."

Jess nodded to draw him out, not trusting her voice to remain steady just yet.

"Bet on the ex," Randy said. His tone conveyed the disgust only the well-informed would feel. "Real piece of shit. Restraining orders, my ass."

Nobody needed to tell her how inadequate the law was at protecting women from men like Richard.

"Can I go up?" *While my legs will still carry me?*

He shrugged again, nodded, as if to suggest there was no harm she could do at this point. "Why not?"

"Who's primary?" she asked.

"Jerry Schmidt. Missing persons."

Jess shivered in the morning's cool breeze, wishing she'd pulled her sweater from the back seat. She made her way down the short street to the brick colonial at the end. She saw two unmarked cars, an ambulance, and people milling around. Officers, crime scene technicians, photographers.

A couple of detectives interviewing a woman, maybe one of the neighbors, maybe the one who'd called in the gunshots. Tallish woman, mid-forties probably. Hair gathered at her nape. Very pregnant. She made a mental note to interview the woman later, if she needed to.

Jess walked up the sidewalk to the threshold and stared into the open front door.

Betsy Martin's body lay on the tiled foyer floor, clad in a neon yellow nightgown, eyes open, frozen in surprise. Two entrance wounds were visible in her chest and abdomen. Lots of blood had pooled. Bullets probably severed the femoral artery. No way Betsy would have survived, even if she'd been found immediately. The thought was little comfort. Betsy's body had been there a while, long enough for all the blood to have congealed. Jess closed her eyes briefly and offered a silent prayer. For Betsy, Anna, and herself.

She moved carefully through the foyer. A few feet inside, Jess caught Detective Schmidt's attention.

"I heard you were in town again," he said, a question in his tone that she'd answered too many times before. *Why?* That's what he wanted to know.

"Betsy Martin was a friend. I thought maybe I could help you find Anna," she said. She might have told him the whole story if Betsy was still alive. Now, that's all he needed to know.

He sized her up as if he'd never seen her before, although the two had worked together on a case last year. He might have sent her packing except time was of the essence and an abducted child was their number one priority. He waved toward the body. "Not a pretty scene."

Jess glanced briefly at Betsy, but she'd already seen more than she wanted to.

"There are security cameras throughout the house and grounds." She pointed to the camera hidden in the wall sconce on the side of the front door. When his eyebrows rose in question, she nodded to convey a certainty she couldn't voice. "They might help."

Schmidt seemed to consider something, but after a few moments he said, "We're not through processing yet. Don't touch anything else." He let her pass.

Jess focused on the work. She moved carefully through the kitchen, Anna's room, Betsy's room, and the door that led outside to the attached garage. She located the surveillance cameras she'd insisted Betsy install and removed the memory cards. The cameras recorded in a loop, replacing images every three days. Maybe they'd get lucky.

One of the techs gave her permission to set up on the kitchen table where she'd waited for Richard Martin on that dark night last year. The bright kitchen lights blazed now, bathing modern steel appliances and glossy surfaces that reflected harshly. Uniformed personnel from multiple agencies moved about as if choreographed by Broadway. No mingling, no collisions, but rising noise levels as equipment was moved in and out, evidence was collected, and the crime scene was both secured and processed. No time wasted, either.

Jess opened her laptop, booted up, and slipped the memory card from the kitchen camera into the slot first. The images downloaded quickly. She and Detective Schmidt watched video of the dark kitchen, but nothing more.

"It was a long shot," he said, by way of forgiveness.

Methodically, Jess downloaded data from the other four and continued searching. "Look there." She pointed to the screen. The intruder had come in through the garage door.

"Who is it?" Scanlon asked, as if he truly couldn't guess. A test, perhaps.

"Richard Martin." No surprise and no doubt about it, either. *He's a bold bastard*, she reminded herself. She swiped a palm across her eyes.

Together, they studied the digital images on the laptop screen. She felt a sick *déjà vu* as she watched Richard invade the house, disarm the security system, climb the stairs, enter Anna's room and return carrying the sleeping girl, as he'd done the night Jess had watched him from this very kitchen chair.

"Dammit!" she muttered. She should have forced Betsy to turn Richard in last year. If she had, Betsy would be alive now; Anna wouldn't be missing.

"Look," Schmidt pointed to the image.

She shook off her scolding and watched Richard reach the bottom of the stairs, his body twisted to the right, toward the garage door this time instead of the back patio.

Almost instantly, bright light flooded the foyer with the flip of a single switch at the base of the stairs.

Camera three had captured the entire scene.

Eerily, Betsy stood alive very near the same location she was laying dead now. "Richard!" her voice screeched like an outraged Valkyrie even from the laptop's inadequate speakers. Jess winced.

Anna awakened, looked around, sleepy-eyed, disoriented. "Daddy?" she said, as if she was surprised to be held in his arms. Which surely she was. He hadn't seen her in fourteen months, and the last time was under harrowing circumstances.

"Put her down, Richard! Don't you dare take her out that door!" Betsy's panicked screech instructed.

"Okay." He chuckled, changed direction and strode past her, toward the front door instead.

Betsy grabbed his arm, jerking it from under Anna's legs.

Richard grasped the child tighter, held her close to his chest. Then, in a quick jerk, he yanked his right arm from Betsy's grasp, reached around his back, slipped a .38 from his belt, and shot her twice. The entire maneuver swiftly executed, as if he'd practiced it until muscle memory supplied all needed direction.

Betsy fell to the floor like a crumpled doll.

Anna screamed, "Mommy! Mommy!" and began to thrash wildly.

Richard held onto the frightened girl despite her screaming, thrashing panic. He strode through the front door and out of camera range. Anna's screams faded as he moved further away from the house.

The screen next reflected the empty foyer captured by the fixed lens of camera three. The scene was grisly enough; the authentic sounds were overwhelmingly heartbreaking. Jess could hardly bear to hear it, but neither could she show her feelings to these men or turn away. Betsy endured the pain; Jess served merely to witness.

After an excruciating lifetime of seconds, Betsy's ever-fainter groans simply stopped.

Moments of stunned silence followed from the gathered professionals.

Schmidt laid a hand on Jess's shoulder, perhaps as small comfort. "We'll get a warrant and an APB. Any idea where he's taken the girl?"

Numb, she said, "He's a Canadian citizen. Lives in Toronto. Wealthy."

Schmidt sighed, resignation showing in the slump of his shoulders. "If he gets her to Canada before we catch him, that's a big problem."

"Why?"

"Canada won't extradite him for a crime that carries the death penalty. And we won't waive the death penalty unless he pleads guilty and accepts a life sentence."

Jess's despair suddenly overwhelmed her. She blinked back tears. "I can see that happening all right."

Schmidt nodded. "Sarcasm won't help. There are some alternatives. None are perfect and they all take time."

"You'll understand if I don't think spending the next two years cutting through bureaucratic red tape to get Anna back through channels is a great solution." Her voice broke. She took a few deep breaths to steady herself. Falling apart wouldn't help Betsy. Or Anna. Or Peter. Jess tried desperately not to think about Peter.

She cued up the last of the video again and checked the time stamp on the image. "He's been gone more than six hours. By private plane, he could easily be in Toronto already."

"Private plane?" Schmidt asked.

Jess nodded. Richard wouldn't have risked a commercial flight.

"We'll check the airlines to be sure," Schmidt paused, ran a hand over his bald head. "Otherwise, I'm afraid we're done here, Jess. He's gone six hours. We won't find him inside this country."

"But you're going to try."

"We'll try." He blew a long, frustrated stream of air out of his nostrils. "Of course, we'll try. Is the girl an American citizen?"

"What the hell does that matter?" If Jess sounded like she was spoiling for a fight, it's because she was. The idea of beating Richard to a bloody pulp sounded perfectly delightful at the moment. If he'd been standing in the room, she might have tried it. Most of the others present would have piled on, she was sure.

"We've got a lot of unsolved cases on the books, Jess. More coming in every day. We can't spend our resources tilting at windmills. We'll turn it over to the Feds if we can't do anything else." He paused.

"But?"

Gently, Schmidt said, "But we have to face reality. For Miami PD, this case is probably closed."

Jess felt a slow burn rising from her toes to the top of her hair. Every nerve ending alert. Betsy dead. Anna missing. Richard Martin gone.

Case closed?

Not a chance.

CHAPTER THREE

AFTER THE FIFTH LAP, cold rain pelting her body, punishing her for screwing up, Jess began to feel a bit better. Although her college racing days were long over, running still cleared her head. The rain slid over her wet skin. She completed a turn around the track and kept pounding, one foot and then the other. She used the steady rhythm that allowed her mind to strategize. The problem wasn't finding Richard. Despite what Schmidt had said, locating Richard would be fairly simple. Jess knew where to look. She'd been watching him for years.

Extracting Anna from Canada was another matter entirely. A much knottier problem. Every solution she tested got pounded to bits by her feet on the cinders.

And if she managed it, somehow, then keeping the girl away from Richard in the future seemed impossible. Hadn't Betsy tried to do precisely that and ended up dead?

Jess had briefly considered becoming a lawyer, years ago, after college. But the authorities searching for Peter, and their failure to find him, left her disillusioned and angry with the law's all-consuming workload as well as its compromises and failures.

The system focused on the rights of criminals, in Jess's view, when it should be more concerned with crime's victims.

All these years later, she was glad she'd chosen investigative journalism instead. She'd quickly discovered she loved the work. It satisfied her in a way she'd never expected while she searched for Peter. And it allowed her to work privately for crime victims' rights when she wanted to, unencumbered by the rules lawyers and law enforcement teams were required to follow.

The lifestyle suited her, too. She traveled to research her stories, but she carefully selected worthy subjects and fashioned solutions for victims that protected them as much as possible. People like Betsy Martin and her sister, Bette. The work funded her search for Peter and fueled her resolve. She'd made the right choices, after a rocky start. Every day she prayed she'd turned her life around before it was too late for Peter. But had she?

Jess frowned and shook rainwater from her eyes and Peter from her thinking. *Focus.* Richard would never leave *his* child alone unless he was in prison or dead. There was no middle ground for Anna. Jess must resolve that problem, too. She needed a permanent solution.

Jess ran, one foot and then the other, pounding the cinders, lap after lap, ignoring the wind and rain that chilled her. Her plan resolved, she finished by walking twice around, allowing the icy rain to drench her body. The cool air now felt refreshing because she knew what she was going to do. Maybe her plan wouldn't work. Maybe she'd end up like Betsy. Maybe Richard would win once more. But she had to try. For Peter. She dropped her gaze to the ground and headed into the showers.

CHAPTER FOUR

JESS WAITED LONG ENOUGH for Richard to relax into complacency and Anna to regain some composure before she flew from Miami to Buffalo. At the airport she rented an anonymous-looking gray sedan. She'd rejected a non-stop flight to Toronto. Although faster and easier, she'd be dependent on flight schedules for the return. Since 9/11, airport security had become irritatingly problematic. She'd be required to prove Anna's identity, which would make them easier to stop and trace. No, driving into and out of Canada was best.

Reluctantly, she rejected buying an untraceable gun on the streets of Buffalo. Taking a gun into Canada was a serious crime. Canadian citizens weren't allowed to carry concealed weapons. Even owning them was severely restricted. If she was caught she'd be arrested and probably imprisoned. Anna would certainly be returned to her father. No, the risk was too great. She'd take Anna away from Richard permanently using guile alone. She refused to fail again.

Jess drove to Lewiston, New York, and checked into a mom-and-pop motel. She rented the room for two nights. Tomorrow, she'd test her plan. The following day, she'd execute it.

She slept lightly for four hours, then dressed casually in khaki slacks, pink shirt, blue blazer, and running shoes. She fluffed her curly blonde hair and studied herself in the mirror, pleased by the guileless soccer mom effect she'd created.

It was dark at five a.m. as she drove toward the Lewiston-Queenston Bridge. If he thought about her at all, Richard would expect her to take the shortest route to and from Toronto. She intended to oblige. Drive time was seventy-five minutes, barring construction or heavy traffic.

The border crossing went well. Off season, during the week, the area was almost deserted both ways. Very few travelers meant only one of the two customs booths was open. As in most of the small tourist towns, the Canadian customs officer simply asked her name, nationality, where she was going and when she planned to return. She'd offered the typical tourist's response for a visit to Niagara Falls and paid the toll. He'd waved her through without asking for ID. *May the return be so easy,* she thought, wiping the sweat from each palm onto her slacks.

She reached the private school where her research revealed Anna was enrolled. After circling the block twice to be sure Richard wasn't lurking and didn't have Anna under surveillance, she parked in front. She had a clear view of the playground while waiting for 10:15 a.m. It nagged her that Richard seemed to have allowed Anna out of his control. Was he that sure of himself? Had he arrogantly assumed Jess had given up? If so, he didn't know her at all. That thought comforted more than the alternatives.

At 10:20, a young woman led twenty energetic children out the door to the playground. Jess spotted Anna. When she saw the little girl with the strawberry curls for the first time, Jess's eyes teared. She wiped her eyes with her fingers, willing the tears away. No time for sorrow now. She pushed all emotion aside as luxury. The job demanded her full attention.

Anna seemed quiet and unfocused, but functional. Eyes dull and heavy-lidded, she stood apart from the other children clutching a rag doll under her left arm and sucking her right thumb.

A low flame of denied anger began in Jess's stomach. Anna's parents had been locked into their own rage, unable to put Anna's life first. The child would never be normal again. Anna was a victim of a tragic struggle. All Jess could do now was try to mitigate the damage. And get the bastard responsible. And maybe, someday, make it up to her by uniting her with her brother.

Richard Martin was no kind of father. Never to Peter, and not to Anna, either. The knowledge soothed Jess's guilt only slightly.

Like every good investigator, she'd analyzed the risks, then constructed Plan A and Plan B. Plan A: she and Anna returned home without Richard's interference, luring him back into the U.S. where authorities would arrest him. Plan B provided an alternative if Richard attempted to thwart her. He would be dealt with at the border crossing. At least, in theory.

Yet again, she regretted the decision she'd had to make about the gun and prayed her alternative would work, even though it could cost Jess her own life. She'd no alternatives left.

CHAPTER FIVE

AS ALWAYS BEFORE EXECUTING the final stages of any plan, Jess slept fitfully. Finally, at 4:00 a.m., she gave up the effort. She dressed again in yesterday's costume and launched Plan A.

Jess arrived at the school two hours early and parked down the street, waiting for Anna's arrival. Just before nine, a station wagon stopped. A young woman helped Anna out of the back seat, and held her hand as they walked to the school's front entrance. The woman was gentle with Anna, but Anna demonstrated no affection when they parted. Anna walked into the school, slowly and alone, dragging the rag doll with her. The woman returned to the station wagon and left.

Jess felt anger's slow burn ignite in her gut. Teeth clenched, muscles tense. She willed her breathing and heartbeat's slowing, even pace. Anger now would only interfere with her performance. Another luxury for later.

When the children entered the playground for recess, Jess left her car and strolled over. She called to Anna twice. The child looked up. A broad grin slowly lit her face. Anna loped toward her.

"Aunt Jess!" she said, crying as Jess picked her up and hugged her, too tightly. She felt thinner inside her clothes. Jess's sadness, followed by hot anger, returned and she allowed herself to feel, just briefly.

Within a few moments, Jess had explained to Anna's teacher that Anna had a dentist's appointment and produced a forged note from Richard allowing her to take the child. The teacher looked at Jess carefully, but released Anna, probably in part because Anna continued to hold onto Jess as if she never wanted to let go. Less than fifteen minutes after Jess first saw Anna on the playground, they were driving toward Lewiston. So far, Plan A seemed to be working.

Constantly checking the rearview mirror, she retraced the route she'd taken the day before. Anna, securely belted in the back seat, had returned to her subdued behavior. She talked quietly to the rag doll she'd brought along with her. About an hour into the drive, her eyelids closed, her chin gently touched her chest and she fell into the rhythm of sleep. A bit of drool slid from the corner of her mouth onto the doll's head. She was so young, so sweet. So undeserving of this mess. Jess clenched the steering wheel so tight her hands cramped.

Was Richard controlling Anna with medication of some kind? Another thing to despise him for. Jess glanced at her watch. Just like yesterday, she was right on time. Even the weather cooperated.

When they approached the border crossing, Jess located the passports, prepared to show them if she had to. She'd seen no sign of Richard or anyone following her for the entire return trip, which worried her.

Richard was crazy, violent, controlling. She'd expected him to know where Anna was every second, and to come after her.

Or at least, Richard should have learned Anna was abducted and reasoned that Jess would take the shortest route back to the U.S.

So far, she hadn't seen Richard. But her senses were on alert. She'd finally learned never to underestimate him. There was something she'd missed. Somehow, she believed, when they reached the border, he'd be there. Then what? She'd already decided. Plan B. Could she pull it off?

Supremely focused now, she drove over the bridge without noticing the spectacular views of Niagara Gorge. At the U.S. check point, the line of vehicles moved swiftly through a single open kiosk. She looked into the cinder-block customs building, which also housed the duty free store. She saw one officer behind the counter, and one clerk in the store waiting on a customer.

While she watched, the customer carried a bottle of liquor in a plain brown bag to the rusty battered panel van waiting in line in front of Jess's vehicle and got in. The panel van belched smoke when it backfired, and its muffler had long ago surrendered to the rust belt.

Mid-week, off season, at lunch time, the entire area was relaxed, thinly patrolled and almost deserted. She hoped this would make Richard more obvious, if he appeared and tried anything.

Jess mentally rehearsed the lie she'd tell if the customs officer asked her more than routine questions. Yesterday, the process was casual, easy, intended to encourage tourism, not to thwart a kidnapper. Would it be the same today? *Please, God.*

Two cars ahead passed through the checkpoint. Only one more ahead of her. When the panel van jerked toward the kiosk window, Jess pulled up and waited at the yellow line. The van blocked her view of the officer.

She glanced around the entire vicinity and saw nothing unusual. Then, looked again toward the duty-free store. She saw a lone figure, vaguely familiar, standing outside.

Could it be?

Richard.

He'd shaved his head and wore sunglasses. But it was him. Definitely. He couldn't disguise his arrogance.

She didn't know how he'd found her, but he had and she wasn't surprised. She'd expected him, knew he'd come. But how?

A tracking device on Anna somewhere? Regular calls to the school just to check on his daughter?

However he'd managed it, he was here now. She had to move. Adrenaline made her heart pound and sweat bead on her brow. No choice now. Plan B.

Stay calm.

Checking the rearview, she realized she'd have to move forward. An eighteen-wheeler six feet behind blocked any alternative, even if she'd wanted to leave the line and return deeper into Canada. Which she didn't. What she needed to do was leave the country. Now.

The officer in the kiosk seemed to be chatting too long with the occupants of the panel van. But she couldn't see the officer and he couldn't see her. She tapped the steering wheel impatiently with her thumbs.

Mimicking the guy who'd joined the van earlier, Richard strolled toward her car. Quiet panic fluttered in her chest as she watched him. Did anyone else see? He reached her car door, looked directly into her eyes as if to mesmerize her, grasped the handle, and lifted it.

The locked door didn't open. He glanced then into the back

seat where Anna slept, covered by the blanket Jess had brought, still holding the doll. The normal sarcastic smirk creased his face. Insight struck.

It was the doll. That's where he'd hidden the tracking device.

Bastard. You think you're so clever. We'll see.

Jess lowered the back window and Richard stuck his left hand on the top of the glass, gripped as if he might pull the glass out. His right hand gripped the passenger door handle.

"Go away, Richard, while you still can. If you try anything here, border patrol will kill you. Your choice."

He laughed. "I'm touched that you'd care. Truly. But you're kidnapping my daughter, Jess. Do you really think they'll take your side over mine?"

While he held onto the glass and the door handle Jess punched the accelerator. The car leaped forward. Richard lost his balance. She slammed the brake. The car's quick jerk threw him to the ground. Her actions, and Richard's, were blocked from the customs officer's view by the panel van, which moved forward now, slowly, through the open gate.

Maybe surveillance cameras saw him. Surely, the border guards would protect her and the child. She hoped.

The officer inside the booth waved her ahead. She released a breath and eased to stop next to the booth, left hand on the wheel.

"What's your citizenship, ma'am?" the kindly old officer asked.

"U.S." She glanced in the right side mirror. Richard had risen from the ground. His stare carried a malevolence she could feel. *Bastard. Go away. While you still can.*

The customs officer glanced into the back seat now, too,

where Anna slept. At the same time, he noticed Richard, hands in the oversized pocket of his sweatshirt, standing too close, not moving, saying nothing.

The officer became more alert. "How about the child, ma'am?" Another officer came out of the building, hand on his gun, waiting.

They *had* seen Richard try to enter her car. It was working. Plan B was working. *Thank God.*

"U.S., too." Small rivulets of sweat tickled her armpits. *Let us go, Richard, and live to try again.*

"Picture I.D., Ma'am?"

Jess reached into her handbag, retrieved the passports and handed them to the officer. He examined the blue jacketed folders. "Your name is Jessica Kimball? And hers is Anna Martin?"

"Divorce," she said. Richard simply stood there. What was he thinking? Was he willing to die to thwart her?

The big truck behind her seemed to breathe fire through its roaring engine when the driver tapped his accelerator impatiently. Jess felt the heat rolling toward her.

The officer glanced at Richard again. Maybe experience, or training or something gave him an uneasy pang. Now, his full attention was focused on the situation. "Do you have the child's birth certificate?"

Jess furrowed her brow with mock consternation. "I didn't think you'd need it."

He closed the passports and gestured toward the building. "I'm sorry, Ma'am. Park over there and go inside where they'll verify your identification." Then he nodded at Richard, who stood stock-still, feet braced shoulder width apart, hands still inside his big front pocket. "Do you know him?"

Now. Plan B. Now was the time. *Do it!*

She took a breath. Exhaled. "He's got a gun."

Before the officer could react, Richard slowly extracted his hand from the sweatshirt, and pointed the gun at her head.

"Get down! Get down!" the officer shouted, squatting beside the car's engine block, the only place safe from gunfire.

In that instant, Richard chose death.

The deafening noise of shots rang out. Bullets entered the rear glass. One grazed Jess's arm as she fell sideways. Another exited inches from where her head had been an instant before. The pain seared through her as blood soaked her blazer and ran down her arm. Anna began to scream.

Border guards acted immediately. They shouted for Richard to drop his gun. He didn't.

A guard shot and hit Richard in the leg. He went down, and kept shooting.

Bullets tattooed the back of the sedan. Anna's screams intensified.

Idiot! You'll hit Anna!

After an excruciatingly long few moments, the customs officer in the booth drew his weapon, and two additional officers ran out from the building. "Drop your gun! Drop your gun!"

Jess looked into Richard's eyes. Either of them could have changed things at that moment.

But they didn't.

Plan B. She jammed the accelerator to the floorboard. The sedan lurched forward, broke through the wooden gate, and raced onto American soil.

Richard shot at Jess's car again. As she'd known they would, the guards returned fire.

Jess mashed the brake, jerking the sedan to a stop behind the solid walls of the U.S. Customs station. Applying pressure to her throbbing, bleeding arm, she managed to open the back door and unsnap Anna's seatbelt. She slid the hysterical child onto the pavement and held Anna close, shielding her, until the deafening gunfire stopped.

In the brief silence, Anna's screams became wailing sobs. Jess struggled to rise while holding the girl despite the searing pain in her arm, and stumbled back to view the scene at the kiosk. Richard lay on the ground, blood running from his mouth, lifeless eyes staring straight at her. Her first thought was, *Thank God.*

Jess's anger flared. He'd chosen to die rather than let Jess take Anna. He'd intended to get all three of them killed. Instead, Peter's father breathed life no more.

At that moment, Jess felt no remorse. Maybe she would be sorry some day, when Peter asked, "Why did you let them kill my father?" But not now.

CHAPTER SIX

A FEW DAYS LATER, Jess joined Bette, who sat watching
Anna on the Land of the Dragons playground. The family
resemblance was unmistakable. Both were clearly from Betsy
Martin's gene pool. In Anna, Jess saw some hint of Richard too.
How could a wonderful child have emerged from two such
damaged parents?

The woman Jess had seen outside Betsy's house the night of
the shooting was there, too. Maria Gaspar's youngest daughter
and Anna were friends. Both girls were on the playground.

"She looks happy, doesn't she?" Bette asked, with a wistful
tone. Anna was in counseling and taking medication which the
psychologist hoped would help her to work through the traumas
she'd endured at her parents' hands.

To reassure her, Jess said, "Don't worry so much. She's
young. With luck and love, she won't remember most of it."

A tear rolled down Bette's cheek. Her lips quivered. "She
won't have much to remember about her mother."

Jess closed her eyes against tears of her own. She had
risked her life so that Anna might thrive. Now, all she

could do was hope. "It's up to you to keep Betsy alive for her."

"We'll help, too, Bette," Maria said, giving Bette's shoulders a hug and meeting Jess's gaze over Bette's bowed head. "Carlos has been like a father to Anna for a while now, anyway."

Jess nodded her agreement to this imperfect arrangement. Together, they watched Anna climb the rope ladders and slide down the dragon's tail, laughing when she landed on her butt in the sand.

"Betsy was so smitten. And he loved her, too." Bette stopped, bewildered. "What went wrong?"

Jess rubbed her sore arm to stop its pulsing. Like Richard's effect on Anna, Jess's wound would hurt for a long time and leave a permanent scar. Jess needed no reminder of the hole in her heart where Peter lived, but welcomed the pain and would welcome the scar, too. She'd narrowly escaped Richard twice. She never intended to forget that, or to make the same mistake again.

She rejected sweetening the truth. To defeat Richard forever, Bette must do her part. "Betsy knew he was dangerous before she married him. She ignored her instincts and deceived herself. I'll help you, but the best thing you can do for Betsy now is to make sure Anna doesn't repeat that pattern."

And I'll be watching.

THE END

ABOUT THE AUTHOR

Diane Capri is the *New York Times*, *USA Today*, and worldwide bestselling author.
She's a recovering lawyer and snowbird who divides her time between Florida and Michigan. An active member of Mystery Writers of America, Author's Guild, International Thriller Writers, Alliance of Independent Authors, and Sisters in Crime, she loves to hear from readers and is hard at work on her next novel.

Please connect with her online:

Website: http://www.DianeCapri.com
Twitter: http://twitter.com/@DianeCapri
Facebook: http://www.facebook.com/Diane.Capri1
http://www.facebook.com/DianeCapriBooks

If you would like to be kept up to date with infrequent email including release dates for Diane Capri books, free offers, gifts, and general information for members only, please sign up for our Diane Capri Crowd mailing list. We don't want to leave you out! Sign up here:

http://dianecapri.com/contact/

THE REACHER REPORT:
March 2nd, 2012

…THE OTHER BIG NEWS is Diane Capri—a friend of mine—wrote a book revisiting the events of KILLING FLOOR in Margrave, Georgia. She imagines an FBI team tasked to trace Reacher's current-day whereabouts. They begin by interviewing people who knew him—starting out with Roscoe and Finlay. Check out this review: "Oh heck yes! I am in love with this book. I'm a huge Jack Reacher fan. If you don't know Jack (pun intended!) then get thee to the bookstore/wherever you buy your fix and pick up one of the many Jack Reacher books by Lee Child. Heck, pick up all of them. In particular, read Killing Floor. Then come back and read Don't Know Jack. This story picks up the other from the point of view of Kim and Gaspar, FBI agents assigned to build a file on Jack Reacher. The problem is, as anyone who knows Reacher can attest, he lives completely off the grid. No cell phone, no house, no car...he's not tied down. A pretty daunting task, then, wouldn't you say?

First lines: "Just the facts. And not many of them, either. Jack Reacher's file was too stale and too thin to be credible. No human could be as invisible as Reacher appeared to be, whether he was currently above the ground or under it. Either the file had been sanitized, or Reacher was the most off-the-grid paranoid Kim Otto had ever heard of." Right away, I'm sensing who Kim Otto is and I'm delighted that I know something she doesn't. You see, I DO know Jack. And I know he's not paranoid. Not really. I know why he lives as he does, and I know what kind of man he is. I loved having that over Kim and Gaspar. If you haven't read any Reacher novels, then this will feel like a good, solid story in its own right. If you have...oh if you have, then you, too, will feel like you have a one-up on the FBI. It's a fun feeling!

"Kim and Gaspar are sent to Margrave by a mysterious boss who reminds me of Charlie, in Charlie's Angels. You never see him...you hear him. He never gives them all the facts. So they are left with a big pile of nothing. They end up embroiled in a murder case that seems connected to Reacher somehow, but they can't see how. Suffice to say the efforts to find the murderer, and Reacher, and not lose their own heads in the process, makes for an entertaining read.

"I love the way the author handled the entire story. The pacing is dead on (ok another pun intended), the story is full of twists and turns like a Reacher novel would be, but it's another viewpoint of a Reacher story. It's an outside-in approach to Reacher.

"You might be asking, do they find him? Do they finally meet the infamous Jack Reacher?

"Go...read...now...find out!"

Sounds great, right? It's available. Check it out and let me know what you think.

So that's it for now ... again, thanks for reading THE AFFAIR, and I hope you'll like A WANTED MAN just as much in September.

Lee Child